The
Crystal Keeper

Sammie realized it was the sound of voices, gentle and clear, like the ringing of small golden bells. She thought dreamily that she had never heard anything so enchanted in her whole life. Then, with a shiver that ran right through her, she realized what they were saying:

"Sammie, Sammie, Sammie!"

She couldn't believe her own name could sound so beautiful.

"Sammie, Sammie, Sammie!"

It was as if a million tiny fingertips were brushing the nape of her neck.

"We need you, we need you, we need you!" Now there was a note of urgency...

The

Crystal Keeper

James Jauncey

For Sophie and Ellie – with all my love

Scholastic Children's Books
Commonwealth House, 1–19 New Oxford Street,
London WC1A 1NU, UK
a division of Scholastic Ltd
London ~ New York ~ Toronto ~ Sydney ~ Auckland

Published in the UK by Scholastic Ltd, 1996

Copyright © James Jauncey, 1996

ISBN 0 590 13339 X

All rights reserved

Typeset by TW Typesetting, Midsomer Norton, Avon

Printed by Cox & Wyman Ltd, Reading, Berks.

10 9 8 7 6 5 4 3 2 1

The right of James Jauncey to be identified as
the author of this work has been asserted
by him in accordance with the Copyright,
Designs and Patents Act, 1988.

Contents

PART ONE

Chapter 1

The Mere

It had been a peculiar dream, the one she'd had last night. Most peculiar, thought Sammie.

She was sitting in the warm sunshine on the wall outside the village shop, eating an ice-cream. It was only now, in a quiet moment, that the dream had come back to her.

The oddest thing about it was that she could picture none of it and yet she clearly remembered the sense of being on the brink of something terribly important – as if she might be about to go and do something that would change the whole world. But what it was remained a mystery. Try as she might, she could remember nothing in the dream that gave her any clues.

There was a clatter as the shop door was flung open and a plump boy in a back-to-front green baseball cap came striding out. Behind a pair of round wire-framed glasses, his eyes were screwed up in a scowl that made him look as if he'd swallowed a wasp. Sammie's heart sank as he marched towards her.

"It's gone," he said sullenly.

"What's gone, Mick?" She tried to sound breezy but his scowl deepened.

"What d'you think's gone, idiot? What I came all the way here for. That water-blaster thingy. The one I've been saving for – for weeks." He shook his head angrily. "Matthew got here first."

"Matthew? Your friend – from school?"

"Friend, huh! Creep, more like." He gave her a sideways look and began to rip the wrapper from the ice lolly he was holding. "Anyway, it's all your fault." He let the wrapper drop to the ground.

"Hey, litterbug!" said Sammie, ignoring him. "There's a bin over there."

He shrugged. "So what?"

"So use it."

"Use it yourself."

"No way! You dropped it. You pick it up!" She was beginning to rise to him. Sooner or later she always did.

He slid his foot over the paper. "Make me."

Sammie shook her head, determined not to lose her temper this time. "I'm not going to fight you, if that's what you want."

"Suit yourself. I don't care." He took off his cap and scratched at the tangle of dark, curly hair beneath. "But it's still your fault."

She took a deep breath. "Why's it my fault, Mick? Why does everything always have to be my fault?"

"Because you're always fiddling about – in your usual pathetic daydream. Otherwise we'd've got here sooner."

"Oh! We would, would we? And what were you doing in your room for half an hour when I was ready to go?"

"None of your business."

"None of my business? When I'm waiting patiently downstairs?"

"Well, nothing you'd understand anyway. Not a pea-brain like you."

"Oh, yes? And what's keeping your ears apart, Four Eyes?"

He went quite still, too furious for a moment to say anything. Then he hissed, "Don't call me that!" and marched over to where their two bikes were propped against the wall. He took a flying kick at Sammie's and it fell over with a clatter. He grabbed the smaller one, swung himself on to it and set off down the street, jamming the cap back on his head as he went.

He had gone a little way when he turned and yelled

over his shoulder: "I hope you've still got some money."

"Oh? Why?" Sammie shouted after him.

"Because I said you'd pay for my lolly." He disappeared round the corner.

Sammie stood there for a while and stared after him, seething with anger. Then she picked up the sticky wrapper and put it in the bin. She went into the shop and paid for the lolly, came outside again and righted her bike. The mudguard had a new dent in it.

I still haven't learnt, have I, she thought miserably as she pedalled away from the shop. If only I could manage – just once – not to let him get under my skin. But I never do. It always ends the same way, and I always feel rotten afterwards. Perhaps he does too – but that doesn't seem to stop him. It's not Matthew that's the creep around here...

She turned off the sunlit main street and into a shady lane. At the far end was a stile into the big wood at the back of the village, and the short cut home.

What had she done to deserve a stepbrother like Mick, she sometimes wondered. It was all very well for her mum and Mick's dad. They liked each other and they'd made the decision to be together. But she'd had no choice in the matter – and trying to like Mick was about as rewarding as trying to like a

4

tarantula with toothache. Of course, when she'd first met him – the previous year – and heard about his mother dying and everything, she'd felt sorry for him. She knew how awful it was to lose a parent. Her father had gone off to live with someone else, and although he wasn't exactly dead, he might as well have been for all she heard from him. But even before she and her mum had come to live at number 3 Mere Cottages, she'd begun to suspect that Mick was just using the whole thing as an excuse to get what he wanted all the time, and be generally unpleasant to everyone into the bargain. Now that she'd been here for six weeks, she was certain of it…

On the other side of the stile, a wide, well-kept path wound its way through the wood for a quarter of a mile and eventually emerged just behind Mere Cottages, almost at the end of their garden. Sammie lifted the bike across the stile and set off again through the trees. With her mind still full of dismal thoughts about Mick, it was several minutes before she looked up and saw that she was on a stretch of path she didn't recognize.

She carried on, curious to see where she would end up, and soon the path halted in front of a clump of thick rhododendron bushes. There was a sparkle of water the other side. She propped the bike against a tree and pushed through the bushes to find herself at the very edge of a little lake.

Surrounded on all sides by the wood, it was about the length of a tennis court but shaped in a crescent, like an untidy new moon. Electric blue dragonflies sailed across the still water like miniature helicopters. A pair of coots scudded busily in and out of a thick bed of reeds on the opposite side.

This must be the mere that the cottages are called after, she thought, sitting down on the sunlit, grassy bank. Although she'd heard several people mention it, she hadn't yet been here. Now she felt pleased to have found the little lake herself, especially since it seemed just the sort of place she liked; a secluded corner she could escape to when people started bugging her, or when she simply wanted to be by herself and dream.

She breathed deeply, feeling Mick begin to slip from her mind. This place seemed almost magically peaceful and unspoilt. For a strange moment, she felt as if she might have been the first person ever to set foot here.

She stretched out on her stomach and gazed down into the water. It was still and clear and she could see a shoal of tiny silver minnows hanging halfway between the surface and the velvety brown silt that covered the bottom. The sun was warm on her back. A pair of cornflower blue eyes gazed up at her from beneath a familiar blonde fringe. She winked and her reflection winked back. Then a breath of wind ruffled the surface and the face and the minnows were gone.

Eventually the ripples spread away and with them, the woodland sounds seemed to fade. In the silence and stillness, Sammie began to feel hypnotized by the wavering patterns of sunlight in the water beneath her.

Gazing dreamily into the mere, it was some while before she noticed that the patterns were beginning to behave rather strangely, bulging and shrinking and sliding together into weird shapes, stretching and straining this way and that, as if they were part of some crazy cartoon. But as her gaze lingered, the shapes seemed to become more familiar and soon, to her amazement, she found herself beginning to recognize things.

There, with only a little imagination, was what might have been a bubbling fountain. It wobbled, then vanished, then reappeared, quite plainly this time, in the centre of a courtyard. A moment later it faded again and in its place came the wavering turrets of a castle with brightly coloured flags a-flutter.

I must be dozing off, she thought. She blinked and

looked again. Now a cluster of red-roofed houses hung perfectly still in the water beneath her, then a farmyard and a duck-pond, then an orchard, so clear she felt she could reach in and pluck a tiny, rosy apple from a drooping branch.

She held her breath in disbelief and pinched herself sharply. But still the images were there, swimming up from the bed of the mere, no longer one by one but all together now, arranging themselves as they came – until suddenly, with a whoosh that took her breath away, she was soaring out like an eagle over a strange and unfamiliar landscape.

Far below her stretched a long, narrow valley with a glittering lake. On every side rose high, white mountains, jagged as dragon's teeth. At one end of the lake, nestling beneath the mountains, stood the castle whose turrets she'd seen. It was surrounded by a little red-roofed town. Beyond the town, fields and meadows stretched along the lake shore until they were swallowed up in the tangle of a dense, dark forest.

Sammie found herself thinking of some tiny, forgotten kingdom that the Crusaders might have chanced upon as they marched to their holy wars; a high, hidden realm where knights jousted in the shadow of the snowy peaks; where maidens sailed the lake in boats as graceful as swans, and young men hunted wolves and wild boar in the forest; where farm lads gathered hay in the meadows beyond the town walls, and lords and ladies feasted in the great hall of the castle.

This can't possibly be happening, protested Sammie's brain. But her eyes told her it was. So did the strange little tugging in her heart that seemed to say she knew something about this extraordinary place. And so, too, did the sound which now began to reach her ears. It was distant at first, no more than the whispering of a breeze. But as it gradually gained strength, Sammie realized it was the sound of voices, gentle and clear, like the ringing of small golden bells. She thought dreamily that she had never heard anything so enchanted in her whole life. Then, with a shiver that ran right through her, she realized what they were saying:

"Sammie, Sammie, Sammie!"

She couldn't believe her own name could sound so beautiful.

"Sammie, Sammie, Sammie!"

It was as if a million tiny fingertips were brushing the nape of her neck.

"We need you, we need you, we need you!" Now there was a note of urgency.

Sammie sat bolt upright and looked about her. For a second she saw nothing. Then she realized that out over the sparkling water, against the blue sky overhead, in the shade of the trees behind her, the air was dancing with brilliantly coloured lights, like the tiny bright stars on the tips of a thousand gemstones. And still the voices called.

"Who are you?" she cried. "What do you want?"

But the voices just kept calling her name.

"Who *are* you?" she cried again.

There was silence for a second and then, as one, the voices drew breath:

"We are the Lights of…"

At that moment another sound intruded:

"Sammie, Saaaaammie!" There was no mistaking her mother's call.

For an instant Sammie felt as if she was being dragged away from this moment of enchantment and back into the real world. But she resisted, making herself concentrate on the voices, closing her ears to everything but the wonderful sound.

"It's all right," she said softly, "I'm still here."

"We are the Lights…" they began again, and again her mother's voice broke in, closer now:

"Sa-man-tha! Lunch-time!"

"Oh, drat lunch!" Sammie muttered to herself.

"Please go away, Mum. Please, please!"

Once more she forced herself to concentrate. The lights had begun to dim now and for a moment she thought the voices had gone. Then she heard them again, ever so faintly:

"We are…"

This time her mother's voice interrupted loudly and clearly:

"Sammie, where *are* you?"

"Oh, no," she sighed. Tears of frustration brimmed as the dancing lights grew ever more dim. "Don't go! Oh, please don't go!"

But it was no use, for suddenly they were there no longer. For a moment, she felt as if the most precious, most beautiful thing in her life had been taken away from her. There was a dreadful, empty ache inside her, and it was all she could do not to plunge into the mere in pursuit. But eventually she took a deep breath, scooped some water on to her face and scrambled to her feet.

"Coming, Mum!" she yelled.

She pushed her way through the rhododendrons and climbed on to her bike. Before she'd even had time to think about it, she found herself back on the main path through the wood, pedalling reluctantly for home.

Chapter 2

A Mystery

"How did you know where I was?" asked Sammie, walking into the kitchen.

Her mother looked up from the stove. "Not difficult. Mick only got back a few minutes ago. He'd taken the short cut. I guessed you'd be in the wood too." She smiled knowingly. "So what was it this time? Birds' nests? Badgers? Bike problems? Or just daydreaming?"

Sammie was about to tell her mother what had happened when a voice inside her whispered: "Don't say a word. No one must know." So she shrugged and said:

"Nothing really. I was just … er … seeing how close I could get to a rabbit. Where's Mick?" There were only two places set at the kitchen table.

"In his room." Her mother pulled a face as she ladled soup into two bowls. "Said he wasn't hungry. He's in a dreadful mood. Sometimes I just don't know what to do with him." She shook her head wearily. "Did you have another row?"

Sammie told her about the scene in the village. "It wasn't my fault, Mum. Well, not to start with. But he always ends up making me so mad I can't help myself. He does it on purpose, you know. I think he likes seeing me lose my temper. Anyway, eventually I called him Four Eyes – again…"

For a moment her mother looked as if she was about to giggle. Then she pursed her lips and sighed. "I know. It's no laughing matter. Specially not for you. You do seem to get the worst of it. But … well … we've got to remember that things *were* pretty difficult after his mum died."

Sammie nodded. "Being looked after by all those different people?"

"Yes – with his dad having to spend all his time looking for a new job. And hardly having any money…" Her mother shook her head.

"I know, I know," said Sammie. "But Mum – that was all five years ago! He was only four then. He's nine now. Shouldn't he have started to grow out of it? Surely he can't still be feeling sad or lost or lonely – or whatever it is. He's got us, hasn't he?"

Her mother nodded thoughtfully, then looked across and said: "But you see, Sammie, I think that may be part of the problem. Perhaps he didn't want us. Perhaps he didn't want anyone else to come along and get between him and his dad."

"Well it's time he got used to it, then," said Sammie crossly.

"I'm afraid not. You can't force things like that," said her mother. "It won't happen overnight. We've just got to try and be really patient." She took Sammie's hand. "You will, won't you?"

"I'll try, Mum," said Sammie doubtfully.

Throughout the rest of the meal, Sammie found she was only half listening to her mother. Her mind kept returning to the mere. As soon as they'd finished and cleared the plates away, she made an excuse and went up to her bedroom. She desperately needed to be alone, to think.

Had it really happened or had she just been dreaming? Maybe it was because she'd been so angry with Mick and her feelings were playing tricks on her. But why hadn't she told her mother about it? If it had just been a daydream, she would have enjoyed watching her mother's face as she described the fantastic things she had seen. Also – the thought only struck her now – according to her mother she'd arrived home just a few minutes after Mick. But how? Either he'd been bicycling very slowly, which was most unlike him because he usually pedalled everywhere as if pursued by a pack of wolves, or something funny had happened to the time while she'd been at the mere. It had certainly felt like more than a few minutes.

She climbed on to her bed and closed her eyes. Then she took a deep breath and tried to reason with herself.

It's nearly the end of the twentieth century, she said to herself. I'm a normal girl called Sammie – well, Samantha, really. I'm eleven, nearly twelve in fact. And a few weeks ago, my mum and I came to live with my new stepdad and stepbrother in their cottage in an ordinary English village. I quite like the new school I'm at, although a couple of the girls in my class drive me bananas, and most of the boys are pretty painful – but not as painful as Mick, which is something. Anyway, I'm good at English and geography and drawing, but I'm lousy at maths and I can't remember the dates in history. I like reading and riding my bike and listening to music. And normal people like me don't see pictures coming out of the water and dancing lights in the air and hear voices calling their names. That only happens in books or on TV. Maybe I'm going mad.

She rolled on to her side and found herself staring

at the clutter of possessions on her bedside table. Amongst them was a photo she'd been given as a leaving present by friends at her last school. There were eight of them, all grinning and waving and making silly faces for the camera. It reminded her of happy times and made her laugh. She specially liked the frame it had come in, because around the large oval space for the main photo were four smaller ovals. Into these she'd placed pictures of her mother; another friend who'd been left out of the main photo; Sammie herself, dressed up as a Hallowe'en skeleton; and her mother's mother, the only grandparent Sammie had known.

Gran had died when Sammie was six – nearly half her life ago. But sometimes, if she looked long enough at the smiling, elderly lady in the photograph, she could still conjure up the memory of a twinkling sort of presence, a faint perfumey smell, and a voice that always seemed to wrap her round with understanding and warmth.

"What do you think, Gran?" she asked now. "Am I going mad?"

Although she expected no reply, she suddenly had the very strange sensation that her grandmother was indeed going to answer her. For a long moment she stared at the photograph, not even daring to blink.

Then, just as suddenly, the feeling was gone and in its place came another, so powerful and unexpected that Sammie almost cried out. It was the sensation from the previous night's dream, flooding back into her, much stronger now, filling her with a sense of utter certainty that something extraordinary and special had happened at the mere.

She got off the bed and began to pace the bedroom floor. She found she was hugging herself, as if to make sure that the precious discovery couldn't escape from inside her.

"I must go back," she said aloud.

Clouds had been gathering since lunchtime and now the air was heavy with the warning of thunder.

As Sammie left her bedroom, there was a loud rumble. By the time she reached the foot of the stairs the downpour had begun and the rain was fizzing and crackling off the flagstones outside the front door.

For a while she gazed dismally out of the hall window. Muted sounds from the sitting room suggested that her mother had her feet up in front of the television. Not wanting to disturb her, Sammie went into the kitchen, only to find Mick sitting at the table, peering through his spectacles at a half-made model aeroplane and several puddles of glue. He said nothing and didn't look up, but she could tell from his expression, and from the way he twisted the little pilot off the plastic stalk and jammed him into the glue-spattered cockpit, that there might be another explosion at any minute.

Why couldn't he have stayed in his bedroom? she thought as she left the room. Why did he have to pollute the kitchen with his foul mood? She found herself picturing one of those big, bad-tempered-looking fish she'd once seen at an aquarium. A groper or grouper or whatever they were called. She could imagine Mick opening his mouth to say some-thing nasty to her and, instead of the usual words, a stream of bubbles pouring out. It made her grin, despite herself. She took her waterproof off the peg by the back door and went outside to the shed in the garden where the bicycles were kept. She would fit the new saddle-bag she had bought and give her bike a good clean. That would keep her busy for a while.

Inside the shed, the sweet, woody smell of pipe tobacco mingled with the tang of creosote and lawn clippings. Old Mr Hobbs, their next-door neighbour, was sitting under the far window on an upturned seed box, peering into the lawnmower.

"Hi, Mr Hobbs," she said, pleased to see him as always.

"Hello Sammie," he replied with a smile.

"What are you doing?" she asked.

"Well … I told your dad – that's what 'e is now, isn't 'e – that I'd 'ave a look at this 'ere mower when I'd 'ad a moment. Blinkin' old thing's on its last legs, if you ask me." He paused and pointed with his pipe. "My, that's a nice bag you got there."

Sammie nodded. "It's new. I came out to fit it."

"Not goin' cyclin' surely? Not in this weather?"

"No. It's just something to do. I was getting bored inside."

"You get bored easy today, you youngsters," said Mr Hobbs, shaking his head. "When I was a young 'un we knew 'ow to make our own fun. 'Ad no choice."

"What sort of things did you do?" asked Sammie. She enjoyed hearing the old man's stories, and it would help pass the time until the rain stopped. Sure enough, he tapped out his pipe on the side of his boot and a distant look crept into his eyes. Sammie drew up another seed box and sat down.

"Takin' a boat out on the mere at night and tryin' to snare a rabbit," he said. His voice had become dreamy, as if he could still hear the oars dipping into moonlit water and feel the noose tighten around the rabbit's throat. "That was fun, all right!"

"But why did you need a boat to go snaring rabbits?" asked Sammie.

"'Cos the biggest, fattest rabbits for miles around lived in a great big warren out on the island! Used to be 'unnerds of 'em till the myxomatosis killed 'em off. And of course, the old fox wouldn't go swimmin' over there, not unless 'e was starvin', would 'e. So they was perfectly safe and they bred like anythin'. Oh, they was beauties, they were."

Hang on a minute, thought Sammie. An island? She was pretty sure there was no island where she'd been this morning. So perhaps she hadn't been to the mere after all – or at least not the main one that the cottages were called after. Perhaps there were several in the wood and she just hadn't heard about them...

"Which mere was that?" she asked.

"Why, this 'un of course," said Mr Hobbs, pointing with his pipe towards the wood. "Only mere around 'ere that I know of."

Sammie's heart missed a beat. Maybe the island had sunk. She'd read somewhere about islands that appeared and disappeared again. But that was in the Pacific Ocean, not here in the middle of England.

Now Mr Hobbs was looking at her in mild surprise. "'Aven't you bin there yet?" he asked.

Sammie shook her head, hoping he hadn't noticed

her confusion. "Just hasn't been time, I s'pose," she mumbled.

"Oh, well, it's a wunnerful place," said Mr Hobbs, back in his youth again. "Right smack bang in the middle of the wood. Did our courtin' there, me and Lily. Used to play skimmin' stones of an evenin'. I always won but she married me all the same!" He chuckled at the memory.

"But is it the same now?" asked Sammie.

"Yes it is," Mr Hobbs replied. "Rabbits are gone, o' course, but nothin' else has changed. You should get your dad to take you there. The boat's still there and I think 'e 'as a key to the boat'ouse – 'e certainly used to."

Now Sammie went cold and goose-pimply. An island *and* a boathouse. There had been neither at her mere, she was certain of it.

"And that's the only mere in the wood?" She tried to make the question sound innocent. "There are no others, no little ones?"

Mr Hobbs gave her a peculiar look. Sammie felt sure he could hear her heart pounding inside her chest. Then he answered:

"Not that I ever 'eard of. But there could've been I s'pose. Could've silted up and grown over, mebbe. Why do you ask?"

"Oh … I was … just looking at a book about the village." The words seemed to appear in her head. "It had some old maps in it … and one of them showed two lakes, one big one and one little one."

"Oh, well, that would be it then, wouldn't it," said Mr Hobbs, all trace of suspicion gone from his face.

Phew, thought Sammie. That was pretty close. She fixed on the saddle-bag as quickly as she could, then said:

"I'd better go now. Mum's going to make cakes this afternoon and she asked me to give her a hand."

"Off you go then, my lass," said Mr Hobbs with a friendly wink. "And tell your mum to save some for me. She's got a grand touch with the bakin'!"

"Okay, Mr Hobbs," said Sammie. She went back into the house, her mind whirling.

Chapter 3

The Whirlpool

Her mere did not exist!

It was well after midnight and Sammie was still wide awake. She lay in the darkness and wondered yet again how she could possibly have been to a lake that had dried out and been swallowed up by woodland many years ago. And that story about the book and the old maps – where on earth had that come from? It was almost as if someone had planted it in her mind at the very moment she needed it.

Feeling very confused, she got out of bed and pulled back the curtains. The rain had stopped at dusk and now it was a clear, starry night. A half-moon cast shadows across the garden. Could she slip out now and go looking for her non-existent mere? No. She was a creature of daylight. The darkness, even moonlight, made her feel timid and uncertain. But early next morning it would be different. She would go at first light while everyone else was still asleep.

She drew the curtains again and got back into bed. She set the alarm for five o'clock and put it under her pillow so that it wouldn't ring too loudly – it would be a disaster if she woke Mick. Then she lay down and closed her eyes.

"I'm going back," she whispered to herself. "First thing tomorrow morning."

She was half awake when the alarm went off. She fumbled under the pillow for the stop button. It was already daylight. She got out of bed and tiptoed to the window. The air was still. A light mist hung over the garden like smoke, and the lawn was almost white with dew.

She trembled a little as she dressed in jeans, a T-shirt and an old sweater. Then she crept downstairs, put on her shoes in the kitchen and slipped quietly outside. There was something thrilling about being up this early, when there was no one else about. Her footsteps felt light and springy as she walked down the garden towards the gate into the wood, leaving a trail of perfect prints behind her.

But no sooner was she amongst the trees than all the confusion came crowding back again. The mere didn't exist. She'd dreamt everything that had happened yesterday. Even if the mere did exist, how on earth was she going to find it? Would she ever recognize the turning she'd taken the day before? No, because it wasn't there…

For a moment she was distracted by the angry chattering of squirrels. Two of the little grey animals were clinging to the trunk of a tree above her, their heads a short space apart. It seemed that one was trying to invade the other's territory.

Eventually the invader gave up and scampered off down the trunk. Sammie looked back to the path and was astonished to see a thick clump of rhododendrons ahead. There was the familiar glint of water the other side. And yet she had thought she was still on the main path to the village…

With her heart beating wildly, she pushed her way through the bushes and stopped. There was the little grassy bank, now sparkling with dew as the sun climbed over the treetops. There were the reeds and there in the middle was one of the coots, tail up in the water. There was no sign of an island or a boathouse.

She ran to the bank and hurled herself down on the grass, ignoring the dew which at once began to soak through her jeans and sweater. She wriggled for a moment to get herself comfortable, then took a deep breath and stared down into the water below her.

For some minutes nothing happened. But just as disappointment was beginning to set in, the pin-points of sunlight dancing on the water before her suddenly blossomed into a million brilliant colours, like the tiny fragments of a rainbow. A moment later the water swirled and as it cleared again she gasped with delight. There, between the high, white moun-tains lay the valley, the lake, the castle, the forest – just as she'd seen them all the first time. She almost cried out for joy.

Then a strange thing happened. The long, narrow valley began to turn like the propeller of an aero-plane. Slowly at first, then faster and faster it spun until all the colours and features were quite blurred and she could see nothing but a whirling disc of brilliant white light.

Sammie began to feel giddy. She was about to tear her eyes away when suddenly the disc shrank until it was no bigger than a penny. All around it, in rushed the water of the mere, swirling and dark, a seething whirlpool with a tiny speck of light beckoning at the very bottom.

Now there was a rushing sound in Sammie's ears. It grew louder and louder as she realized that she was beginning to tumble down into the whirlpool, spinning and cartwheeling, over and over, round and round.

I must be dying, she thought, for a brief moment. And then she heard the voices. "Sammie," they cried, "we need you." The black walls of the whirlpool dropped away. The rushing sound ceased and she was floating peacefully downwards through soft, clear light.

Sammie found her eyes closing, her mind and body relaxing, and then there was nothing.

She could hear water lapping gently, just in front of her face. She opened her eyes and blinked in puzzlement. It was dark. Could she have dozed off at the mere and stayed there, asleep, all day? Surely not!

She got to her feet and looked around. As her eyes grew used to the darkness, she became more confused. This wasn't the mere. This was some high, mountainous place. She was by a little lake, lying in a hollow between the brow of a hill and a steep, rocky shoulder.

She shivered. Where on earth was she? And why was it dark? For a moment her mind seemed unwilling to work. Then, in a flash, came the memories of the spinning valley, the dark whirlpool and the bright light.

So this must be the other side, she thought, the fear coming all in a rush now. She strained her eyes into the darkness, hoping to see some sign of life – approaching lights, maybe. But there was nothing. Only the unruffled black waters of the little lake. With a horrible panicky feeling, she sat down again and put her head in her hands. If only Mum was here to tell me it was just a dream, she thought. If only I had someone with me, even Mick…

In time the panic passed. She took a deep breath and tried reasoning with herself. Here I am, she said, on an unknown mountainside. I suspect it's by the valley I saw in the mere, but I don't know yet for certain. I've no idea why I'm here and I haven't a clue what to do next. But if I am where I think I am, it was the dancing lights and the voices that brought me here. They were beautiful things. Surely they couldn't mean me any harm? So, if they've gone to all the trouble of getting me here, they're not going to leave me sitting on a mountainside as soon as I arrive. Someone will be on their way to find me…

Although it was reassuring to think things through, Sammie still felt very uneasy, and the darkness didn't help. It might be better if she was actually doing something, she thought. She got to her feet and at that moment there was a glimmer as the rim of the moon slid up from behind the mountains.

She started walking towards the brow of the hill, then stopped as the dim shape of an animal appeared, making its way across the shadow of a large boulder in front of her. Only when it came out into the moonlight did she relax. It was nothing but a common hare.

The hare made for the skyline, then turned round and sat back on its hind legs, its eyes glinting in the moonlight as it looked directly at her. Sammie waited a while, but it stayed where it was so she took a pace forward. To her surprise the hare still made no move. She began to get the uncomfortable feeling that it was trying to prevent her from going forward.

This is ridiculous, she thought. It's only a hare. She held its gaze and marched straight towards it. Not until she was very close did the hare eventually drop to all fours and lollop away.

Now she hurried to the brow of the hill and stopped, peering out into the night.

She was standing high up on a mountainside with steep, rocky slopes tumbling dizzily away into the darkness at her feet. Far below, a ribbon of water shimmered in the moonlight. Beyond, all was in deep shadow, except for the distant twinkle of lights, away at one end of the water, and opposite her, the outline of tall jagged mountains rising dimly against the stars.

If I believe what I'm seeing, she thought, this could be Austria or Switzerland or any other country where there are valleys and mountains and lakes.

But there was something else – no more than a whisper on the warm night air – that told her it was neither of these, nor anywhere else she'd ever find in an atlas. And all of a sudden she knew, without any doubt, that this was the place she'd seen in the mere – a place full of such magic that it made her heart flutter and the hairs stand up along her arms. Now she no longer felt frightened. She was filled, instead, with a tingling sense of wonder at what had happened.

For a long time she stood in a trance and stared into the night, until at last her mind began to turn again. Where was this place? And why was she here? Had she travelled back in time, or forward into the future, or even sideways into another world…? With these and a thousand other questions tumbling through her head, she began to pace restlessly up and down, peering across the darkened mountainside in the hope that someone would soon come to her rescue.

Chapter 4

Shadows in the Dark

As the moon rose higher and higher and still no one came, Sammie began to grow frightened again.

She stopped pacing and stood still for a moment, wondering whether she should try and find a way down to the lake, or climb around the shoulder of the mountain to see what was on the other side. But before she could make up her mind, something huge and silent sailed overhead, blotting out the moon and casting a deep, midnight shadow on the ground. Sammie shivered with dread as she heard a flutter of wings behind her. Slowly she turned her head and there, a short distance away, stood an enormous owl.

Her insides turned to ice as she stared at the giant bird and it stared back at her. It was as big as a man, snowy white from the top of its head to the tip of its tail. Its great beak curved out to a needle point and its talons looked as sharp as knives. From inside their

31

wide feathered circles, two huge black eyes gazed out unblinkingly.

It could tear me apart in a second, thought Sammie, trying not to move a muscle. But the owl just stood there, quite still, and as Sammie looked a little more closely she noticed that its shoulders were drooping and it seemed altogether rather weary. She began to get the feeling that it meant her no harm.

She waited a minute longer, then took a hesitant step forward and was startled to see the owl give a little jump. She was even more startled, a moment later, to realize that it had begun to speak to her. It was a strange kind of speaking. The great beak remained shut and there was no sound to be heard, but the black eyes seemed to spring to life and words began to form in Sammie's mind. As she understood them, it was all she could do not to laugh out loud with relief.

I'm sorry, he said, *but you gave me a fright then.*

"You gave me one, too," said Sammie.

Oh, I know, I know. He shook his head. *I keep doing it. Don't mean to … but, well … I haven't really got used to being an owl yet.*

That was a peculiar thing to say, thought Sammie. Whatever did he mean? She was about to ask, when he went on:

You see, if I speak to people straight away, they don't

get so alarmed. But – I'm a bit out of breath tonight. I've been all over the place.

"Looking for me?" she asked hesitantly.

He nodded. *You'd never believe how difficult it is to find your way round these mountains in the darkness, even for an owl. Well … for me, anyway.*

"So you know who I am?" said Sammie.

Of course, of course! He grew flustered. *You must forgive me. This – this owl business – it makes me forget my manners. You're Sammie! Welcome to our valley, Sammie!*

"Thank you," said Sammie. "And thank you for finding me."

The owl nodded, then sighed. *Everything's such a rush tonight. Now I've got to get you straight to the castle, as quickly as possible.*

"Why?" Sammie began – and all at once the questions came flooding back. "I mean, why am I here? And where is here? How did I get here?"

The owl shook his head. *I'm afraid I'm not allowed to tell you, Sammie. All I can say is that it's very urgent. And there's someone at the castle who'll be very pleased to see you – and explain everything, I promise. So, come on now, we must be on our way.*

"Those lights I saw," said Sammie, pointing into the distant darkness, "were they the castle?"

The owl nodded.

"But it's miles. I can't walk that far. Anyway, isn't it the other side of the lake?"

Again the owl nodded.

"So how are we going to get there?"

Almost before the words were out of her mouth, there was a strange sinking in Sammie's stomach and she felt as if her feet had left the ground. She looked up and caught a moonlit twinkle in the great dark eyes.

"We're going to fly!"

He nodded.

Sammie could have sworn he was smiling.

When you're ready then, he said, and set off for the brow of the hill. There he stretched up on his toes, opened his wings wide and flapped them hard. They made a whumping sound as they beat the air. He did this several times, as if it was some kind of exercise or practice. He seemed quite lost in what he was doing.

"Excuse me," said Sammie eventually, "but what d'you want me to do?"

He turned round, still flexing his wings, and looked at her.

"I mean … you're not expecting *me* to fly as well, are you?" she asked.

He shook his head vaguely.

"Well then, if you're going to carry me, I need to get on to you somehow."

Now he looked confused.

A nasty thought sidled into Sammie's mind. "You have … um … done this before, haven't you?" she asked.

Hrrm, said the owl, then glanced around briskly and pointed with one wing at a large boulder. *There, climb up on that rock, please.*

Sammie scrambled up on to the top of the boulder and waited anxiously as the owl approached. When he was level with her, he turned away and bent forward. Sammie hesitated. Then, with a deep breath, she lowered herself on to the broad, snowy back and twined her fingers deep in the thick down at his shoulders.

Are you all right? he asked.

"Yes," she replied.

Hang on, then.

He took a short step forward and with one long beat of his wings they were sailing up into the night air. For an instant, Sammie felt as if she had left herself behind on the ground. She gasped as they soared out over the crest of the hill and the mountainside plummeted giddily away beneath them. She glanced at the glimmer of moonlit water, far, far below, and for a moment her mind went blank with terror, her stomach turned cartwheels.

Don't look down if it makes you feel funny, said the owl. *First thing I discovered. Always better looking straight ahead – or up, if you prefer.*

Sammie lifted her gaze and the cartwheeling stopped immediately. The night sky was clear and velvety and the moon looked so big she could almost touch it. She was certain that the stars were getting closer. This can't be happening, she found herself saying; but another part of her wanted to sing out with the wonder and magic of it all.

The owl seemed hardly to use his wings at all and they floated along at a gentle pace. Now Sammie felt safer, perched amongst the deep, soft feathers on his back. A warm night breeze ruffled her hair. The owl seemed to be enjoying it too, for although he'd stopped talking, he was making a quiet "ooh-rooh, ooh-rooh", somewhere deep in his throat.

It was a wonderfully soothing sound, thought Sammie, as they sailed through the moonlight. Ooh-rooh, ooh-rooh. Somewhere between the soft hoot of an ordinary owl and the gentle coo of a pigeon.

After a little while, Sammie allowed herself to glance down again. Directly beneath were the slopes, shadowy and treacherous and split with dark chasms which plunged deep into the roots of the mountain. There were yawning cliffs and strange, gnarled outcrops, and everywhere, the gaping mouths of caves. She shivered and turned her gaze across the water to the firefly lights of the distant town.

"Who lives in the castle?" she asked.

But her question went unanswered, for at that moment she felt the owl's body stiffen beneath her, his wingbeat quickened and he turned his head intently towards the darkened mountainside, scanning this way and that.

I'm going to have to put you down, he said. *Hold on tight!* Then they were swooping towards the ground. It was the most terrifying feeling Sammie had ever had. She closed her eyes as they dropped and dropped and the air whistled past them and the mountainside rushed up to meet them. For a dreadful moment she wondered whether he'd lost control. Then there was a bump and they were down.

Sammie slid trembling to the ground and the owl said urgently: *That rock. The big one, over there. Get behind it. Quickly.*

She could tell that this was no time for questions. She ran obediently to the rock and ducked down. All was dark and silent. After a while, she peeped around the corner. The owl was no longer there. Then she looked up and glimpsed his white form hovering by the mouth of a cave, some distance above her head. She could hear a sound, a faint twittering and squeaking, which seemed to come from inside the cave.

The next instant, what looked like a long cloud of smoke came pouring forth and suddenly the night air was filled with the dry rustle of leathery wings and a shrill chorus of high-pitched squeaks. Sammie's knees went weak as she realized that the cave was full of bats.

It's all right, came the owl's voice, faintly. *Just stay where you are. Keep out of sight.*

For some time the bats milled about in the darkness as more and more came streaming from the mouth of the cave. Then, all together, they wheeled and swooped down the mountainside towards her. Sammie shrank behind the rock in terror, just as the owl launched himself at the fluttering horde.

Somewhere not far above Sammie's head, the owl and the bats met. For a moment their downward flight was checked as the owl hovered and the dark stream swarmed around him until he was almost lost to view. Then, very slowly, the swarm began to lift as the owl fought for height.

Sammie held her breath, expecting at any moment to see the great bird fall from the sky. But he battled on and after a while, still heaving and wheeling, the swarm began to drift away along the moonlit mountainside. Sammie caught glimpses of a white wing, the slash of a talon, and a shower of small dark objects dropping earthwards, and she realized what he was doing: he was leading the bats away from her.

She turned away, not wanting to see or even think about what they must be doing to him, and found herself glancing up again at the cave. Its mouth was empty and the air around her was still. She was about to stand up when, from behind her, came a rustle of wings. She crouched down again but it was too late. Something brushed her arm. Something else tugged lightly at her hair. She felt a wingtip flutter past her cheek. And then they were all around her.

"Help!" she screamed, standing up and flailing her arms in terror at the army of shadows that flitted and darted about her. With their tiny sharp claws, their bald heads and little pig-like snouts, they were like creatures from the darkest pit of her imagination.

"Help me! Owl, please help me!" she screamed again. In panic she stumbled this way and that, trying to cover her head and at the same time lash out at her attackers. But only when it was almost too late did she realize that, little by little, the bats had been driving her towards a long, steep, gravelly slope – a slope which ended in thin air, sliced by the knife-edge of a cliff.

She turned to fight her way back to the rock but a fluttering wall of furry bodies and leathery wings closed against her. She took a pace back, then another and suddenly her balance was gone and she was tumbling down the slope.

Down she slid, now head first, now feet first. She clutched for anything that might save her from hurtling out over the edge of the cliff. But her bleeding fingers grasped only flints.

"Oh, somebody, please save me!" she muttered and suddenly, above the sound of her fall, there was a whoosh of wings and with a thud that knocked the wind from her she fetched up against something solid. Choking for breath, she opened her eyes and found that she was lying against the downy legs of the owl. His breast was heaving as he looked down at her, eyes full of concern.

Are you … all right? he asked breathlessly.

At first Sammie felt too shocked to reply. She simply lay on the ground, unable to think or move. But as her senses returned and she realized that the danger was past, she began to feel angry.

"They were trying to drive me over that cliff, weren't they?" she said. "They wanted to kill me."

The owl nodded sadly.

"Well why? Can you please tell me why?"

But the owl merely tipped his head towards the cave. *They won't be back,* he said. *I've made sure of that now.*

"That doesn't answer my question," said Sammie crossly. Still trembling, she climbed to her feet and began to examine herself. Her jeans were ripped across one knee and there was a twinge in her left ankle when she put her weight on it. But to her amazement there seemed to be no serious damage.

"Can't you tell me anything about what's going on here?" she demanded.

I wish I could, said the owl, *but I've already explained...*

Suddenly, Sammie felt on the point of tears. She looked up at him and said shakily: "You ... you saved my life – not just from the bats, but ... from falling over the cliff, too."

With a solemn smile, the owl stretched out a wing and gently drew her to him. Sammie buried her head in his soft down, finally overwhelmed by everything that had happened in these last few extraordinary hours. For what seemed like an age, she sobbed and sobbed and the owl held her close, until eventually there were no tears left and she stepped away with the feeling that she had cried herself clean and light inside.

Only now did she remember how the bats had swarmed around him. She looked at him anxiously. One wing was trailing and there were feathers missing. His whiteness was speckled with blood and he seemed to be limping.

"You're hurt, too," she said.

He gave another grave smile. *It's nothing serious – not for me anyway. It's you I'm worried about.*

"Why?" asked Sammie. "I'm all right, really I am."

He shook his head. *It's not that. It's ... well ... I don't think I can carry you any longer.*

His shoulders drooped, as if he was suddenly ashamed of himself. He looked so troubled that Sammie longed to comfort him, the way he had just comforted her.

She stroked the tip of his wing. "Don't worry," she said. "I'll just have to walk, that's all. I'll manage. You can lead the way."

Are you sure? he asked.

"Of course," said Sammie. "As far as the lake, any-way. Then we might have to think of something else. It looks a bit far to swim to the castle!"

The owl brightened. *There are fishing villages on the shore. They have boats.*

"Well," said Sammie, "that's fine then, isn't it."

The owl nodded. *You're a brave girl, Sammie.* He sounded almost proud. Then, quietly, he added: *Praise the Lights!*

Sammie felt too tired to ask him what he meant. The moonlit water still looked an awfully long way away, and all she wanted now was somewhere she could lie down and go to sleep. But she wasn't going to be able to do that here on the mountainside.

"I suppose we'd better get going, hadn't we?" she said.

The owl nodded. He gave a couple of hesitant flaps, then lifted into the air. With his damaged wing, his flight now seemed awkward and clumsy. But he moved ahead a little and hovered, waiting for Sammie to join him. She saw that he was leading her on to a narrow, rocky path, winding down through the darkness towards the distant water.

The first light was creeping into the sky and they had been going for what felt like hours, when the throbbing started in Sammie's ankle. She gritted her teeth and kept going, but it seemed to get worse and worse until as they finally stepped on to the soft white sand of the shore, there was a shooting pain. She sat down and lifted up the leg of her jeans. The ankle was very swollen. It felt burning hot to her touch.

In a moment the owl was on the sand beside her, a look of sympathy in his great dark eyes. She tried to stand up, but as soon as she put weight on her left foot, the pain shot through her like a knife. She bit her lip to stop herself crying out and sat down again.

"I'm sorry, Owl," she said. "I don't think I can go any further." This is really great, she thought. First the poor old owl can't carry me, now I can't even walk.

Never mind, said the owl, his voice full of sympathy. *It's not far now. Look.*

He pointed along the shore to where Sammie could faintly see the grey shapes of a cluster of huts against the paleness of the lake. Then he moved up close to her and bent forward a little. He stretched one huge wing around her back and under her arm, and lifted it so that when she was standing it supported her like a crutch.

Not quite flying, I'm afraid, he said, taking a step forward.

"Next best thing, though," said Sammie. She could feel the warmth of his body next to hers as together, in the gathering light of dawn, they made their way slowly along the shore of the lake.

Chapter 5

Across the Lake

It was the noise of flapping canvas that woke her. Sammie opened her eyes and looked up to see a dirty brown sail being tugged by the breeze. The air was warm and all around was the sparkle of water. Beyond, high white mountains towered into a brilliant blue sky.

Little by little things started coming back to her. The owl and their wonderful flight beneath the stars. The bats and the terrifying tumble down the mountainside. Then the rocky path and the painful limp along the shore in the grey dawn. She dimly remembered something about some huts as well – but after that, nothing.

Now she was lying in the bows of a little boat, resting comfortably on a pile of sacks. Her injured ankle was stretched out in front of her. Although it still looked very swollen, the sharp pain had given way to a dull ache that she was just about able to ignore. Sitting opposite her was a little nutbrown man wearing a grubby tunic of some sort of coarse cloth. He was whittling away at something with a knife. It looked like a piece of fishbone, but it was too small for Sammie to see what he was making.

As she heaved herself up, he put away his carving and a lopsided smile spread across his face. He poked his finger at his chest and said:

"Jandus."

"Jandus," Sammie repeated. Was he telling her his name?

The little man beamed with delight. Then he pointed at her and raised his eyebrows expectantly.

Sammie placed a finger on her own chest and said: "Sammie."

"Sa…mi," said Jandus hesitantly.

Sammie nodded.

"Sa-mie!" he said more confidently.

"Yes. Good!"

Jandus beamed again and clapped his hands together.

"Uru bring Sa-mie to Jandus."

What on earth did he mean?

"U-ru," Jandus repeated. "Ooh-rooh, ooh-rooh." He flapped his arms. "Ooh-rooh, ooh-rooh."

Sammie smiled as she understood. Her thoughts

turned fondly to the great white owl. So much seemed to have happened to them in such a short time.

She nodded. "D'you know where he's gone?"

Jandus shrugged. "Fly, fly." He flapped his arms again, then pointed over Sammie's head.

She turned round to see that they were making for the end of the lake. Directly ahead, like poppies around a large, dusty stone, the red roofs of the little town clustered about the castle. A green patchwork of woods and meadows spread back along the opposite shore as far as the forest. And in the background, ringing the entire valley with their treacherous slopes and jagged, snowy peaks, were the mountains.

For a fleeting moment, Sammie had the uncomfortable feeling of being imprisoned in this deep, narrow place with its forest and lake and castle. But in the same instant she knew there was something magical about it. She'd felt it last night on the mountainside, waiting to be rescued. Now, in broad daylight, the feeling was much stronger.

It was as if all her senses had been sharpened. The air tasted and smelt deliciously clean and pure. The light seemed incredibly bright and clear. Even at such a distance, she felt she could almost see in through the castle windows, sink down into the deep grass of the meadows, lose herself in the darkness of the forest.

Strangest of all, though, was the tingling sensation. Sammie had never drunk champagne, but from what she had heard people say, she imagined that this must be what it was like – millions of tiny bubbles fizzing away inside her, filling her with some miraculous energy. Or perhaps it was more as if she'd swallowed a great gulp of the tiny, multi-coloured sparkles that had danced around her at the mere.

"Sa-mie like soup?" Jandus's voice broke into her thoughts.

"Ooh, yes please," said Sammie. She was absolutely starving, she realized.

Jandus smiled and felt at his feet to produce a little beaker and a clay pot. He poured some of the pot's contents into the beaker and passed it to her, then smacked his lips loudly and grinned.

Sammie took a sip. It was a fish broth, hot and a little salty. She took another sip, then another, feeling its warmth and goodness starting to spread through her.

The air also was growing very warm. She glanced up to see that the sun was directly overhead and realized, with a start, that she must have been in this land for at least twelve hours. Was time the same here as at home? If it was, her mum would be mad with worry by now. For a moment she felt the panic returning as she imagined her searching the house, dashing through the wood and calling her name, then ringing the police, combing the fields and country lanes...

Oh, Mum, she thought, I love you so much and I wish I could let you know I'm all right so that you won't worry about me. But there's really nothing I can do. So I'll just have to hope that when I do get back, you'll forgive me and I'll be able to share my secret with you.

For some reason this silent conversation with her mother made Sammie feel better at once. It was as if her thoughts had been carried away on the wind to that other time and place called Mere Cottages. A picture of her mother, contentedly asleep, came into Sammie's mind.

"Sad Sa-mie?" inquired Jandus, a note of concern in his voice.

She felt a little wary of saying too much yet. "Just thinking..." she replied. "Jandus, did Uru tell you why I'm here?"

Jandus rolled his eyes and spread his hands, as if to say: Why ever would he tell a simple fisherman like me a thing like that?

"But you do know where to take me?"

This time he smiled his lopsided smile. "Castle!" he said proudly. "Uru say…" He glanced up as something caught his eye.

Sammie followed his gaze to see a large black bird circling high above them, its wings outspread. The smile had left Jandus's face and he was drumming his fingers nervously on his knee.

"What is it?" asked Sammie.

Jandus seemed to have lost his voice. He stared up as if he could no longer take his eyes away, while the bird circled lazily lower and lower. Sammie also felt her gaze being drawn towards it. The longer she looked, the more uncomfortable she felt. It was a huge raven, its blackness like a stain on the perfect blue of the sky, a drop of poison settling through the pure, clear air. And when a rasping croak rang out, shattering the stillness of the lake and echoing away across the mountains, Sammie's blood ran cold.

"Wh-what does it want, Jandus?" she asked.

But Jandus still could not speak. The huge bird was not far above them now, hanging in the air currents directly over the boat. Sammie could clearly see the ruff of feathers at its throat, the cruel black beak and the sharp little eyes staring at her as if they could peel away her thoughts like the layers of an onion. She longed to burrow down into the bottom of the boat, out of sight – but now, like Jandus, she could no longer take her gaze away.

At last, just when she thought she could bear it no longer, the raven gave a lazy flick of its wings and drifted away across the lake in the direction of the forest.

For a while they sat there, saying nothing. Sammie gripped the sides of the boat so that Jandus wouldn't notice how much her hands were trembling. Jandus seemed intent on avoiding her eye.

Then a breeze sprang up. With a look of relief, Jandus at once set about trimming the sail. Soon the little craft was scudding across the lake towards the town.

Sammie asked him again:

"What did it want?"

But Jandus shook his head as if to say that he could not, or would not, answer her. Then he gestured ahead to the castle and its family of little red-roofed houses and exclaimed:

"Soon we come! Soon we come!" He held out the soup-pot with a flourish. "Now, more soup, yes? Good things in soup for poor leg!"

Sammie gladly took it and poured herself another beakerful. The soup was lukewarm, but it still tasted good. There was a tang of herbs in it which she'd been too hungry to notice the first time. Perhaps it did have some remedy in it. It certainly helped to calm her.

When she'd drunk her fill she settled back. The dwindling dot in the sky had at last disappeared against the darkness of the distant forest. She looked across the water to the little town, the castle – and the answer, she hoped, to the questions that were once more beginning to buzz around in her head like a swarm of restless bees.

Chapter 6

Helio

As they drew closer, the town seemed to grow bigger, spreading out around the harbour in a sunlit jumble of red roofs, whitewashed walls and brightly painted shutters and doors. Now Sammie could see people bustling about on the quayside and strolling through the maze of narrow cobbled streets that climbed towards the castle. She even thought she could glimpse figures on the battlements. Voices carried faintly across the water.

Jandus steered for a handful of fishing boats and moored alongside them. As he took down the sail and stowed it away, Sammie watched the comings and goings on the quay. The tingling feeling had returned, and with it, that extra sharpness and brightness to everything she could see around her. It was as if she'd stepped into a film, she thought, as her eye fell on a group of weather-beaten fishermen mending their nets, a pair of scruffy kittens playing tug-of-war with a piece of twine, a stream of porters carrying crates and bales on board a pair of larger sailing ships, one with deep scarlet, one with emerald green sails.

When Jandus had finished his preparations, he squatted down in front of Sammie and fumbled inside his tunic, then held something out and pressed it into her hand.

"You take," he said. "From Uru. For luck!"

She looked down to see the little piece of fishbone he had been carving earlier. It was a tiny white owl, perfect in every detail.

"Did Uru ask you to make this for me?" she asked, with a shiver of delight.

Jandus nodded proudly.

"It's beautiful!" she said. "Thank you, Jandus. Thank you very much!"

Jandus blushed. He reached into his tunic again and took out a thin leather thong which he threaded through a little groove in the owl's back. Then he held it up to Sammie's throat. She took the ends of the thong and fastened them around her neck. Now Uru will be with me all the time, she thought.

Jandus smiled happily, then helped her from the boat and gave her his arm to lean on as they set off along the quay. Sammie noticed that the fishermen and porters, and the one or two other people who had now come down to the harbour, were all wearing tunics or robes of one kind or another. She began to feel very self-conscious in her ripped jeans and sweater. Sure enough, as she drew level with the fishermen, their conversation stopped and they looked at her curiously. As soon as she was past, there was muted laughter. She could feel her ears going red. Jandus quickened his pace.

It was only then that Sammie realized her ankle had almost stopped throbbing. It felt just a little stiff. She stopped and gingerly put her full weight on it. There was hardly even a twinge.

"That soup seems to have done the trick," she said. "My ankle's much better."

"Good medicine soup," Jandus replied, nodding his head.

They left the harbour and began to climb a cobbled lane with washing hanging from windows and birds twittering under the eaves. A little boy with a dirty face sat in an open doorway, his eyes wide as saucers as he watched Sammie walk past. She heard him calling for his mother to come quick and see the funny lady.

At the top of the lane they paused before a broad street lined with brightly coloured stalls of all shapes and sizes. A deafening throng of men, women, children and dogs were barging, jostling, scuffling and scampering in all directions. Carts rattled and groaned over the cobbles. Somewhere a sheep was bleating. There was an almost overpowering smell of cooking and spices.

Jandus glanced uncertainly from side to side. Then he made up his mind and plunged into the crowd.

Sammie took his arm again as he fought his way down the bustling street. The sights and sounds and smells of the market made her senses reel. Now she felt not so much as if she had stepped into a film, but tumbled into a kaleidoscope. For a moment her head swam and she thought she might pass out, but she gripped Jandus still tighter and struggled on, trying to ignore the curious stares.

Eventually they found their way blocked by a crowd who were noisily laughing and applauding at some spectacle. Dragging Sammie behind him, Jandus elbowed his way through the mass of bodies. They emerged at the front to see three acrobats ending their performance in a flurry of handsprings and cartwheels.

There was a moment's hush. Then two men appeared, one carrying a drum and the other leading a bear by a chain attached to its ankle.

Aahh! went the crowd as the great brown animal lumbered into the ring, its chain clinking on the cobbles. When they reached the centre the drummer began to tap out a rhythm: rat-tat-a-tat, rat-tat-a-tat. To the crowd's delight, the bear broke into a shuffling dance. It swayed from side to side and lifted its huge shaggy paws one after the other, in time with the drumbeat.

As it danced, the bear moved slowly around the ring. When it reached the place where Sammie and Jandus stood, it suddenly stopped.

"Get on, you!" grunted its owner, giving it a prod. But the creature refused to budge. Its huge head waved slowly from side to side and its nostrils twitched as if it were scenting something.

Then it took a pace forward and stopped again, directly in front of Sammie. Slowly it lowered its head until its eyes were level with hers and it was staring straight at her. The drummer stopped playing and the crowd fell silent.

Sammie's blood ran cold. The bear was trying to stare her down, just as the hare had done, back there on the mountain. But there was something much more frightening about this creature – not just because it was bigger, but because of the mean, hostile look in its piggy little eyes.

Sammie found herself edging back. Her heart was thumping and she knew that she should get away as fast as she could. The bear took a pace forward and she could stand it no longer. She turned and fled.

The bear lunged after her, jerking its owner off his feet. For a moment he held on to the chain. Then, as he began to be dragged along the ground, he let go. At once the crowd broke in panic, screaming and yelling, pushing and shoving as everyone fought to get out of the way.

"Jandus!" Sammie yelled, but she was trapped in a heaving sea of bodies and her cry was drowned by the noise around her.

For what seemed like an age, she was carried along by the multitude, struggling not to fall and be trampled underfoot.

When at last the stampede slowed and the crowd thinned, Sammie stopped in a doorway, breathless and shaken. She looked about her in dismay. She was in a narrow, gloomy alleyway. At each end there were other little streets, equally narrow and dingy.

Jandus was nowhere to be seen.

For some moments Sammie stood still, catching her breath and trying to work out where on earth she was. Then, feeling suddenly furious and rather frightened at the same time, she banged the doorway with her fist.

"I've really had enough of this place," she said out loud. "I'm supposed to be in the castle by now –

getting answers to everything. And instead I'm lost. Chased into the back streets by a bear." The sound of her own voice made her feel better. "What's up with the animals here? Do I smell funny or something? And where's Uru for that matter? If he can find me up a mountain in the dark, surely he can find me here? Well, I'll show them. I'll find my own way to the castle and tell them just what I think of this horrible uncivilized dump."

"It's not really that bad, you know."

Sammie almost jumped out of her skin. She looked up to see a boy standing in front of her. He must have crept up on me, she thought.

"I wish people would stop giving me frights," she said crossly.

"Sorry," said the boy.

He was a little bit taller than she was, but about the same age, and he looked as if he'd just crawled through a hedge. His robe was torn and stained, his bare arms and legs grey with dust, and there were bits of straw in the tangle of dark hair that fell almost to his shoulders. But in his deep blue eyes, there was a wicked glint which said that whatever he'd done to end up looking like this, he'd enjoyed every minute of it.

Now he was looking at Sammie very directly. He

seemed to be weighing her up. If he says anything about my funny clothes, she thought, I'll scream. But he didn't. He merely asked:

"Did you say you wanted to go to the castle?"

"Yes, I did," she replied.

"I'll take you." He sounded very matter-of-fact about it.

"You will? Are you sure?"

"Yes, I'm sure."

Sammie hesitated for a moment, wondering whether she should trust him.

The boy threw out both arms and smiled an irresistible smile. "Follow me!" he said.

Sammie found herself stepping out of the doorway and setting off after him. Their footsteps echoed in the narrow, dingy alley.

"Why d'you want to go to the castle?" he asked, as they reached the end and turned into another little street just like the one they'd left.

"I'm not really sure," said Sammie, not wanting to say too much. "At least I am, but – well – it's all – a bit complicated. Let's just say I've got to meet someone."

"Of course," said the boy, as if he was always taking people to the castle to meet someone.

Now they seemed to be winding their way deeper and deeper into a rabbit warren of tiny alleyways.

Sammie looked up, hoping to catch a glimpse of the turrets and battlements, but all she could see around her were crowded red rooftops.

"You do know where you're going, don't you?" she asked anxiously.

The boy nodded. "Trust me."

I haven't got much choice, thought Sammie.

"What's your name?" she asked.

"Helio," said the boy. He grinned, as if deciding whether to let her in on a secret, then said: "And you're Sammie."

Sammie stopped in amazement. "H-how do you know?"

"Easy." He pointed at her clothes, his grin widening. "Anyway, everyone knows. They're all out looking for you, right now."

"Who?"

"Everyone. The Master, the Dame, the servants, the castle guards."

The Master and the Dame. They sounded important, thought Sammie. "So you knew that's where I wanted to go all along," she said.

He nodded.

"Why did you ask me, then?"

For a moment he looked almost serious. "Because we have to be careful these days."

Careful of what? Sammie was about to ask, then thought better of it. If Uru wasn't allowed to tell her anything about what was going on here, there certainly wouldn't be any point asking this scruffy-looking street rascal.

Instead she asked: "Were you looking for me, too?"

"Hmmm … well … not officially…"

Now he stopped by a wooden door set into the wall of the lane. He pushed it open and stepped inside. Sammie followed him into a little courtyard and was surprised to see him heaving aside a big flower tub. Beneath it there was an opening in the ground. She watched in growing dismay as he began to lower himself down into it.

"Am I supposed to go down there too?" she asked, eventually.

He halted with only his shoulders sticking out. "Of course. I'm taking you to the castle."

Sammie looked at him uncertainly. "Is this some kind of joke?"

The twinkle left his eyes and he sounded almost hurt as he replied: "No, Sammie. Come on, it's quite safe."

But Sammie had stopped listening. Why was nothing straightforward in this wretched valley? she thought. Why did she have to get lost? Why did it have to be some kind of ragamuffin who found her? And why on earth did she have to go down a hole in the ground to get into the castle? She hated being underground – it made her feel all peculiar.

"Is that the only way in?" she asked sharply. "Isn't there a proper front door, or gates, or whatever castles usually have?"

Helio heaved himself back out of the hole and stood up, looking rather sheepish. "Yes, of course there is," he said. "It's just that this is … my special way in."

"Ahh…" said Sammie, nodding to herself. "Now I get it. Special – because if you tried to get in the front way, they'd kick you straight out again."

"That's not…" Helio began to protest, but Sammie ignored him and went on:

"I expect you're really a burglar. You certainly don't look like anyone who ought to be in a castle."

"Well you're wrong," Helio retorted, his eyes flashing angrily. "I am. In fact, if you really want to know, I'm the Master's son. And the Master – for your information – is the ruler of this valley. So if you want to meet him and find out why you're here, you'd better follow me."

With that he scrambled into the hole again and disappeared.

Chapter 7

The Castle

Oh, help, thought Sammie, as she climbed slowly down the ladder into the darkness. If he's telling the truth, that means he's some kind of prince or something. And now I've gone and offended him.

At that moment she heard him reach the ground, then the echo of his departing footsteps.

"Wait!" she called in sudden panic. "Don't leave me here! Please!"

The footsteps stopped. She heard a match being struck and immediately there was light below her. She looked down to see Helio walking back towards the foot of the ladder, holding a lantern.

"I wasn't going to," he said with a grin. "Just fetching the light." He held out his arm as she stepped to the ground, then waved proudly around him. "So what d'you think? My very own tunnel! Hasn't been used for years. I'm the only one who knows about it now."

Sammie shivered. "I'm not very good at tunnels." She peered into the darkness ahead. "Is it far?"

"Only a few minutes." Helio held up the lantern and smiled encouragingly. "Come on, then. To the castle!"

Sammie took his arm, glad of the excuse to stay close within their little pool of lanternlight. As her eyes grew used to the light she could see that it was more of a passageway than a tunnel, about half as high again as she was, and just wide enough for the two of them to walk side by side. Even with the lantern and Helio beside her, she felt uncomfortable, as if the earth was pressing down on her. To keep her mind off it, she said:

"Can I ask you something?" She had to speak quite loudly to be heard above the ring of their footsteps.

Helio nodded.

"If you're the Master's son, and the castle's your home…"

"…why do I come and go like a rat?" Helio finished her question with a chuckle. "I don't always. But sometimes, for a punishment, I'm not allowed to go out. And then … well … I don't like being kept inside…"

"I see. So you sneak out through your secret tunnel. Then what?"

"Oh, hang about with my friends in town. Hope no

one spots me. Play a few jokes on people. Go down to the harbour. You know the kind of thing…"

If I close my eyes, thought Sammie, I could be listening to any one of the boys I know at school.

"How did you get so dirty?" she asked, then added anxiously: "Or is that bit still to come?"

Helio laughed. "No! Don't worry. It happened in town."

"How?"

"I jumped over a wall without looking to see what was on the other side."

"That was silly. Why?"

"Because – well – there were some people who weren't terribly pleased with me…"

"And?"

"I was being chased."

"Why?"

He paused. "Pinching their goat. At least that's what they thought. Actually, I just wanted to see if I could milk it."

"And could you?"

"Couldn't even catch it!" He grinned ruefully and rubbed his backside.

Sammie giggled. "I'd like to have seen you! Anyway, how did you find me?"

"Luck really. I happened to see all the commotion

in the marketplace – with the bear and everything – and I just had a hunch… Look, we're almost there now."

A set of stone steps rose into the darkness ahead of them. They climbed for a few moments, then halted at the top while Helio fumbled with something. A second later there was a soft creak and a shaft of daylight appeared, together with the strong, orchardy smell of fruit.

Helio snuffed the lantern and they stepped out from behind a huge row of shelves into a larder-like room, full of presses and basins, jars and bottles, and tray after tray of apples, pears, plums and blackcurrants. Sammie breathed deeply. You could make enough jam for our whole village here, she thought, as Helio touched the shelves at one corner and they slid back snugly against the wall.

They left the larder and made their way into the main part of the castle. Here it seemed rather shabby, full of cobwebby passages, worn flagstones and faded tapestries. But it was a friendly kind of shabbiness all the same, with dusty shafts of sunlight escaping through half-open doors and a smell of woodsmoke and baking bread drifting up from somewhere below.

After a few minutes they stopped at the foot of a spiral stone staircase. "Just up here," Helio said.

"One last question," said Sammie. "If everyone was looking for me, and you were the one that found me, surely your parents'll be pleased."

"Mmmm…" said Helio.

"Well then, why didn't we just come in the normal way, through the front gates or whatever?"

For a moment he looked at her quite seriously. Sammie wondered whether she'd said something wrong. Then a grin slid across his face.

"Because it's more fun this way!" he replied.

At the top of the staircase they stopped before a carved wooden door.

"Wait here!" he whispered.

He straightened his robe and ran a hand through his hair – rather pointlessly, thought Sammie, since it was still full of straw – then winked and rapped loudly.

"Enter!" came a man's voice from inside.

Helio turned the handle and went in, leaving the door ajar so Sammie could hear every word that followed.

"Aha! And just where have you been this time, young man?" The voice was stern but pleasant.

"Into town, Father. I know I shouldn't have, but I really thought I might be able to help – to find the Beyonder…"

"But just look at you, Helio…" It was a woman's voice now.

"I know, Mother. I'm sorry. I'll go and have a bath in a minute, I promise. Anyway, have you found her yet?"

"I'm afraid not," the Master replied.

"That's a pity…" Helio paused, then: "I've got a surprise for you!"

"Oh?"

"Close your eyes for a minute."

"I'm not in the mood for pranks, Helio."

"I think you'll be pleased! Go on, close your eyes!"

There was another moment's silence, then Helio appeared at the door. He beckoned triumphantly. Sammie stepped into the room as he commanded:

"Now open them!"

"By the Lights!" exclaimed the Master, looking up.

"Good gracious!" said the Dame. "Is it…?"

"Yes, Mother, it is." Helio was now grinning from ear to ear. "This is Sammie!"

At once the Master and Dame rose to their feet, smiling broadly.

"Welcome, Sammie," said the Master, walking over and shaking her warmly by the hand. "Welcome indeed!" He was silver-haired and tall, but a little bent, as if he'd spent a lifetime banging his head on things. He had a kindly, slightly startled look, and when he smiled, as he did now, his eyes were lost in a hundred creases. He reminded Sammie of someone's favourite uncle.

Now the Dame stepped forward to clasp both Sammie's hands in hers.

"Oh, this is wonderful, wonderful my dear!" she said excitedly. "You've no idea how worried we were."

There was a lovely bubble in her voice that made her sound like a contented pigeon. In fact, she looked a little like one too, thought Sammie. She was short and rather pretty, in a plump, cosy, middle-aged way. But in the round, pleasant face were a pair of huge green eyes that gazed directly at her with a sparkle of magic or energy or some kind of power that made Sammie start fizzing inside all over again. She knew at once where Helio's mischief came from.

"I'm afraid you've had a perfectly dreadful journey here," said the Dame, fussing around her as she led Sammie to a big, soft-looking couch. "You must be very tired."

"And hungry, I expect," said the Master. "I'll order something to eat. Then you can tell us all about it." He tugged at a bell-pull hanging beside the door. There was a faint clanging in some distant part of the building.

"Now just you settle back and relax, my dear," said the Dame, drawing up a little table to Sammie's side. "Goodness knows what you've had to put up with since you arrived." She plumped up a couple of cushions and placed them behind Sammie's head. "Are you quite comfortable?"

"Yes, thank you. I'm fine," said Sammie, sinking back into the couch and looking around her.

This room, like the rest of the castle, had seen better days. It must have been in one of the towers, for it was completely round with windows on three sides. Golden afternoon light streamed across the ceiling-high shelves of books, the scuffed furniture and frayed carpets, the deep old chairs and sofas. But shabby as everything was, there was something so obviously loved about it all that Sammie felt immediately at home. She could imagine them snug and warm in here on a winter's night with the heavy, faded curtains drawn against the frost and snow outside, and logs blazing away in the big stone fireplace.

On the wall opposite her hung a portrait. There were the Master and Dame in their best robes, standing by a sundial in a garden full of flowers. There at their feet, a young Helio was playing with a small brown dog. Standing beside Helio, the Master's hand on his shoulder, was an older boy. He looked a little more serious than Helio, although it was obvious they were brothers. But there was something else about him that seemed strangely familiar, too.

Sammie was trying to work out what, when there was a knock at the door and a servant came in with a tray of food. He put it down on a little table beside her, then walked back across the room and went out. The door had almost closed when there was a loud snuffling and a patter of paws and the little brown dog from the portrait came trotting in. It made its way towards Helio, then caught sight of Sammie and stopped dead. For a moment it bared its teeth and growled. Then, with a furious snarl, it launched itself across the room towards her.

"Toto," cried the Dame, rushing to the rescue, "you wicked thing! How dare you!" But Helio got there first and before the little dog could do any damage, he picked it up by the scruff of the neck, carried it out into the passage, and shut the door firmly.

"Oh, my dear, I'm so sorry," said the Dame. "I don't know what got into him."

"I do," said Sammie quietly. "It's what's happened with all the other animals." She felt suddenly very cold and shaky inside. "Before I go completely mad, will someone please tell me what's going on."

Chapter 8

The Master's Tale

The room was silent as the Master walked across to the bookshelves. He took out some books and unlocked a small secret cupboard set into the wall behind them.

The Dame quietly took her place beside Sammie and slipped an arm through hers. Helio sat down in a chair opposite.

The Master turned round. In his hand was a little glass bottle with a small amount of clear liquid at the bottom. He held it up for Sammie to see and the sunlight caught the glass, throwing dancing patterns on the wall opposite.

"This is what it's all about," he said, tapping the bottle with his finger. He paused for a moment, frowning thoughtfully, then went on: "You see, Sammie, this valley of ours may seem much like any other, but there's one thing about it that's very unusual. We're lucky enough to possess a crystal of great magic..."

"A crystal which has protected us for centuries against evil," said the Dame.

"Yes, it makes an invisible barrier around us," the Master went on. "Nothing can touch us here. Nothing can enter the valley unless we allow it to. And while the crystal protects us from the world beyond, the Dame takes care of what goes on here, inside the valley, with the help of this little bottle."

"How?" Sammie asked. "I mean, what's in it?"

"Crystal water," the Dame replied, "from the pool where the crystal is kept. I use it for spells, to make sure our life is as harmonious as possible…"

"She's really a witch!" whispered Helio.

The Dame smiled and shook her head. "Don't listen to him, Sammie. He's just a ruffian. No – I have no power of my own. It all comes from the crystal water."

"Where is the crystal?" Sammie asked.

"Hidden deep in the forest," the Dame replied, "at the place we call the Crystal Sanctuary. You see, every few years we choose one of our finest young men. He is told how to find the Sanctuary and sworn to secrecy. He vows to go and live there, guarding the crystal with his life, until the time comes for him to be replaced by another. It's a hard, lonely existence, but to be chosen as Crystal Keeper is the greatest honour in the valley.

"Once a year, we meet the Crystal Keeper at a special place at the edge of the forest. He brings us the crystal water and lets us know that all is well…" She paused and glanced at the Master. "But last year, my dear, something went terribly wrong. The Crystal Keeper didn't come."

"Why not?" asked Sammie, beginning to wonder what all this had to do with her.

"We didn't know at first," explained the Dame. "So we sent Helio's older brother into the forest to find out what was happening. Dear, brave Laslo…" Her voice faltered.

Sammie glanced up at the older boy in the portrait as the Master continued:

"When Laslo reached the Sanctuary he found that something dreadful had happened to the Crystal Keeper. He'd gone quite mad. He was ranting and raving – one moment boasting of how he'd mastered the crystal, the next, cursing Laslo for coming to spy on him. Laslo did his best to discover what had happened, but the Crystal Keeper got angrier and angrier and finally hurled a spell at him…"

"We think he meant to do something really terrible," interrupted Helio, "like turn Laslo to stone, or make him vanish or something. But he hadn't really got the hang of the crystal magic yet, and what he actually did was turn my brother into an owl – a great white owl."

"Uru!" Sammie gasped. Her hand went to the little carving at her throat.

The Dame nodded sadly.

As she pictured the owl, Sammie was struck by a sudden thought. "If he's really Laslo, why do some people call him Uru? I mean … I know it's the sound he makes … but isn't it confusing?"

"We didn't want people getting more alarmed than necessary," the Dame replied with a wistful smile. "So we pretended Laslo had gone off on a hunting trip into the mountains, and that Uru was someone completely different who'd come to help us."

"So most people don't know who he really is?" Sammie asked.

The Master nodded.

"I see. So then what happened?"

"Well," said the Master, "now that Laslo was an owl, he could fly wherever he wanted and report back to us what he saw. It certainly wasn't what the Crystal Keeper had intended – but it was lucky for us, all the same. And for a while it seemed that the Crystal Keeper was quite happy practising harmless magic at the Crystal Sanctuary."

"But then…?" Sammie was beginning to get a

nasty feeling about this story.

The Master shook his head slowly. "Then the harvest failed – for the first time ever. Animals started behaving strangely. We began to hear of people disappearing in the forest…"

He fell silent and stared out of the window. After a moment the Dame took Sammie's hand in hers and said quietly: "We love this place, Sammie, this beautiful valley and all the people in it. We'll do whatever is in our power to save it from danger … and we believe the danger may now be very great. That's why we brought you here."

"But what can I do?" asked Sammie, wishing suddenly that she was somewhere else.

The Master looked at her. "Today is the day we go to the forest to collect our crystal water. Crystal Keeper's Return we call it. If, by a miracle, the Crystal Keeper has recovered and brings us the water, the danger will be past and life will return to normal. We'll send you straight home, with our blessings."

"And if he doesn't?" Sammie asked, despite herself.

"Then we'll need your help," said the Dame.

"What will I have to do?" she asked in a small voice.

The Dame patted her hand and said: "Go to the Crystal Keeper and cure him."

*　　*　　*

So that's it, thought Sammie, with a horrible sinking feeling. She clenched her fists and closed her eyes tightly, willing herself to be back at Mere Cottages. But when she opened them again she was still in the sunlit room with the Master, the Dame and Helio looking on.

"Why me?" she asked miserably. "I can't cure him."

"Yes you can," said the Master with a nervous smile, "you have the power to do it. We don't."

Sammie shook her head. "You've got the wrong person. I don't have any power."

"Oh, but you do, my dear," replied the Dame, patting Sammie's hand again. "You'll find it when the time comes, believe me. And because you will never have used it before, it will be pure and strong."

Sammie stared at the floor and shook her head again. This couldn't be happening to her. It just couldn't. It was all a dream. She'd wake up soon and everything would be all right…

She looked up to see the Dame nodding gently, as if she could read Sammie's every thought. Suddenly she felt angry.

"Couldn't you have waited?" she burst out. "I mean, at least till you knew what the Crystal Keeper was going to do."

Now the Dame shook her head. "The Beyond-seeking spell – the one that brought you here – is very difficult to cast. It was the first time I'd done it. In fact, it's only ever been used once before…"

"Yes," interrupted Helio intently, "the Winter of the Wolves. It was one of the most terrible moments in the whole history of the valley…"

"Helio," said the Dame sharply, "this isn't the…"

But the Master glanced at her and said: "Let him go on, my dear. It won't do any harm for Sammie to hear this tale."

The Dame hesitated, then smiled. Helio continued:

"That was the winter it was so cold the crystal pool froze solid. The crystal was trapped in the ice and began to lose its strength. Then the wolves started pouring down out of the mountains. Hundreds of them. No one ever discovered whether it was because the crystal was growing weaker, or just because of the terrible cold – but whatever the reason, the wolves were starving and ferocious. They began to hunt through the valley in packs – even into the streets around the castle – until all the people were in terror of their lives. The Dame, my great-great-great-great-grandmother, tried every spell she knew, but nothing had any effect.

"What they needed, of course, was the power of

the crystal itself. But by that time the snow had drifted so deep around the Sanctuary, it was completely cut off. No one could go into the forest anyway because of the wolves. The crystal seemed to be dying in the ice. And the Crystal Keeper had become too weak from cold and hunger to free it."

"So what happened?" asked Sammie.

"Well, eventually they used the Beyond-seeking spell and brought in a beautiful young Beyonder. Elizabeth she was called. The spell landed her right in the Crystal Sanctuary. Somehow she helped the Crystal Keeper recover and together they got the crystal out of the ice…"

"And…?"

"And…" Helio grinned, "a few days later it began to thaw. By the end of the week there wasn't a wolf to be seen in the valley – and there's never been one since!"

"Whew!" said Sammie.

"Yes," said the Dame, "she was a brave girl, that Beyonder … but no braver than you, Sammie. Anyway, as I was saying, the Beyond-seeking spell is very difficult. It takes a long time to prepare and it needs a lot of crystal water. And that's why if we'd waited until today, to see how things turn out, we might have been too late."

"The Crystal Keeper had already begun to interfere as it was," added the Master. "You must have guessed that we didn't mean to land you halfway up the mountain."

"Hmmm," Sammie said. "All right. So, you've got me here now. And it seems I've got this power that everybody knows about – except me…" She paused and looked up at the Master with his stooping figure and anxious smile. "So, have I actually got any choice? I mean, could you send me home now?"

"Of course we can, my dear," he replied, almost apologetically. "This very minute if you want. It's a two-way spell. It has to be. We could never bring anyone here and keep them against their will. The Dame only has to say the word."

Well, that was something, Sammie thought. And yet … she already felt strangely attached to these people. Master and Dame they might be, but there was also something ordinary and friendly and kind about them. Could she just abandon them? Maybe not. But all the same, just because she liked them, did that mean she should run the risk of what might be mortal danger…?

Her palms were getting clammy and her heart was starting to thump. She didn't want to say no, but her head hurt with all this thinking and she was beginning to feel frightened and confused as well. She closed her eyes and took a couple of deep breaths. Then the Master's hand was on her shoulder.

"It's all right, Sammie," he said gently. "We know how difficult it is. You don't have to make a decision this minute. Let's wait and see what happens."

"Are you sure?" Maybe the Crystal Keeper would come anyway, she thought.

"I'm sure." The Master smiled.

For a moment Sammie felt as if a weight had been lifted from her. Then the Master glanced at the window and raised an eyebrow. "I didn't realize it was so late," he said. "The sun's getting low already. I'd better be on my way."

The Dame stood up and smiled at him. "I'll take Sammie to the spell-chamber," she said. "Helio, you come with us."

"But I always go with Father for Crystal Keeper's Return," protested Helio.

"Not this time," replied his father firmly. He paused when he was almost at the door and said to the Dame: "I think, my dear, that we should get in touch with the Weaver."

The Dame nodded.

"The Lights be with you," she called softly as he left the room.

Chapter 9

Back To Beyond

"**W**ho's the Weaver?" asked Sammie as they turned into a long echoing corridor. The trick was to keep talking, keep asking questions. Then she wouldn't have to think about it all too much.

"He's the oldest man in the valley," Helio answered, "and the wisest. He lives on Oak Holm. It's an island in the lake. If anyone knows what to do, he will."

Mention of the lake reminded her of Jandus and she put her hand up to touch the little fishbone owl again. It felt smooth and warm and strangely reassuring. She was about to show it to the Dame when they stopped before a pair of tall double doors. The Dame threw them open and waved Sammie inside.

Unlike the comfortable, sunlit tower room, this was a large, shadowy chamber with a vaulted roof and a stone floor; the sort of place that made you want to whisper, thought Sammie. A single stained-glass window, high up in the wall, let in a dim, green, underwatery sort of light. Apart from a couple of shelves of ancient leather-bound books, some chairs and a long, low couch, the only other furnishing was a stone basin on a pedestal. It stood alone in the very centre of the room, just like the font in a church, Sammie thought. She looked closer and realized that all around it, a great circle of magical signs had been set into the floor.

She was just deciding that the whole place was rather spooky, when the Dame snapped her fingers, there was a soft hissing from the font and a brilliant rainbow appeared above it. Seconds later the rainbow exploded into a million little multi-coloured sparkles that floated up and hovered near the ceiling like a galaxy of fairy lights.

"That's better!" said the Dame cheerfully. "Can't stand that dismal green light. It always makes me think I've drowned."

"The sparkles!" Sammie exclaimed. "I saw them at the mere!"

The Dame smiled. "The Lights, we call them. They're always there when the crystal water's at work. Now, I must make the font ready so we can see how things go at the meeting place. Helio, while you're waiting, why don't you show Sammie the book about the Winter of the Wolves?"

Helio nodded and went over to the shelves. The Dame turned towards the centre of the chamber and began to take slow, graceful paces around the magic circle, singing in a soft voice and pausing every so often to make a little bow towards the font.

Sammie found herself wondering, more than a little anxiously, what was going on. Could they really be about to watch a ceremony that was taking place in another part of the valley? And if they were, did she want to see it, anyway...?

Then Helio was beckoning her to the couch. She went across and sat down beside him, and he opened the large volume he had taken from the shelves. Sammie realized at once that it had no text, just page after page of beautiful illustrations. And as Helio began to tell the story in his own words, slowly turning from one picture to the next, she soon forgot everything else. She could almost feel the icy cold, hear the howling in the darkness, as she gazed at a mountainside cloaked in snow, a trail of pawprints in the moonlit forest, a terrified face at a lonely cottage window, a man running for his life down a deserted street.

When at last they came to the picture of a young,

fair-haired girl struggling through waist-deep snow towards a frozen pool, a sudden shiver ran up and down Sammie's spine. Helio looked up from the book with a startled expression. He stared for a long moment at Sammie, then looked back to the picture again, shaking his head.

"Extraordinary!" he said in a half-whisper. "You could almost be…"

But at that moment the Dame turned round from the font and beckoned to them. "It's nearly sunset," she said with a small, tense smile. "Time for Crystal Keeper's Return."

Leaving the book on the couch, they stepped up to the stone basin and Sammie saw that it was swirling with a milky vapour which gave off a vibrant glow, like bright moonlight. It made her feel giddy to look at and she was about to turn away when the Dame murmured soft words. The room grew dark as the Lights dimmed. Sammie shivered and stood closer to Helio.

Now there was only the glow from the font and that too was dimming swiftly. But something else was beginning to happen. It seemed as if there were vague shapes of people and trees swimming through the swirling, misty vapour. At the same time the faint sound of voices began to steal through the spell-chamber. Then, suddenly, the mist was gone and Sammie found herself looking down on to a huge crowd of people gathered at the edge of the forest. Before them was a small clearing. In its centre lay a great slab of white marble. It was like an altar, glinting in the dying rays of the sun.

"Thank the Lights!" the Dame exclaimed softly. "I was afraid that we might not be able to see."

Sammie gazed down in fascination, wondering what kind of magic it was that allowed them to look into a simple stone font and see this distant gathering at the edge of the forest.

"Is it the meeting place?" she asked.

The Dame nodded, not taking her eyes from the scene before them.

Now Sammie noticed that the crowd seemed tense and expectant, and all at once she could no longer avoid thinking about what was going to happen. She felt a flutter of panic in the pit of her stomach.

"Please let him come!" muttered Helio under his breath.

Yes, thought Sammie fervently, please, please!

Presently, from the front of the crowd, the tall stooping figure of the Master strode forward. As he reached the marble altar, the sun dipped below the horizon. He turned to face the gathering, raising his arms as he did so, and his voice rang out as clearly as if he was standing in the spell-chamber:

"Good people of the valley, another year has passed and Crystal Keeper's Return is here once more. As always, we have come to give thanks for our glorious crystal and its blessed Lights."

"Praise the Lights!" cried the crowd.

"We have also come to honour our noble Crystal Keeper," the Master declared, his voice as steady as ever, "to receive the crystal water and offer him thanks for the safekeeping of our most precious treasure. So now we humbly ask that the Crystal Keeper come forward."

He turned towards the darkening forest and commanded: "Crystal Keeper, come forth!"

"Come forth!" echoed the crowd.

Distant watcher though she was, it felt to Sammie as if she was right at the Master's side. She held her breath. Seconds passed and nothing happened. The Master stood his ground and issued the command again. Now there was a note of challenge in his voice.

"Come forth!" echoed the crowd again, urgently this time.

Still nothing happened. All eyes were fixed on the forest. It seemed to Sammie as if time was standing still.

Suddenly the Master stiffened. Sammie concentrated her gaze. For a moment she could see nothing. Then there came a great gasp from the crowd and at the same instant she spotted it – a black shadow, snaking out from the forest, creeping across the woodland floor, spreading like a bloodstain as it wormed its way towards the stone. And still the Master stood there like a statue, his arms upraised.

"Move, Father, move!" muttered Helio through clenched teeth.

But the Master was unable to move. In a flash, the shadow had encircled both him and the altar and was slithering forward again towards the horrified crowd. It halted right before their feet and rested there a moment.

Then, with the faintest trembling, it began to swallow up the marble until Sammie could no longer distinguish the great stone from the menacing, inky pool that surrounded it. As the last patch of light vanished, a plume of darkness spiralled into the air and hung there spinning, like an evil little black whirlwind.

Faster and faster it spun until, with a blinding flash, it exploded, the shadow disappeared, and there on top of the offering stone stood a small glass bottle.

"Praise the Lights!" roared the crowd as the

Master stepped forward and reached out tentatively to take the bottle. Then came a great groan of dismay. Sammie clutched Helio's arm to see the Master turn round ashen-faced and empty-handed. Where the bottle had been there was nothing but a tiny mound of dust.

There was a moment's horrified silence, then a demented cackle of laughter seemed to burst from the font and peal through the spell-chamber. Sammie clapped her hands to her ears as the scene before her clouded and a pair of bloodshot, staring eyes began to appear through the mist that now swirled in the stone basin. Wider and wider grew the eyes and beneath them appeared a thin, cruel mouth, parted in a hideous grin.

"Be gone!" The Dame's desperate cry rang out at Sammie's side. She felt Helio grab her and try to drag her away. But her feet seemed rooted to the floor. Try as she might she could not tear her gaze from the eyes which swam in the mist before her and seemed to be boring through her.

Then a roaring filled her ears, she tried to call Helio's name, and there was blackness all around her...

S he was staring into the still water of the mere. Her damp clothes clung to her body. Her head felt thick and woolly, as if she might have fainted. But down in her stomach – for some reason she couldn't explain – there was a tense, frightened feeling. She glanced at her hands and was startled to see they were trembling.

What on earth's going on? Sammie wondered. And why am I here?

For several moments she could remember nothing. Then a jumble of images swam into her mind, and a moment later the whole sequence of events in the valley unreeled in a flash. She sat up with a shiver and looked around her.

The grassy bank still sparkled with dew. A coot paddled about at the edge of the reeds and the sun hung just above the treetops opposite. She glanced down at herself. Her jeans were a little crumpled but there was not a rip to be seen.

It's exactly as it was when I arrived here, she thought, getting to her feet. Could I have fallen asleep and dreamt the whole thing?

Thoroughly confused, she turned her back on the mere and set off for home. As she reached the garden she saw that her footprints still lay clear on the dew-laden grass.

The house was silent. She crept upstairs and froze for a moment as someone stirred in her parents' bedroom. Then she was in her own room, the door safely shut behind her. A soft, early morning light filtered through the curtains. She looked at her rumpled bed, the clothes draped over the chair, the familiar clutter of books and possessions, and felt a great flood of relief.

She sat down on the bed and started to undress. She undid her shoes and took off her socks. She pulled off her jeans and let them drop to the floor. Then she reached up to pull the sweater over her head and as she did so something sharp scraped across her chin. She fumbled inside the neck of the sweater and her hand closed around the little fishbone owl.

For a moment, an extraordinary thrill ran through her. She wanted to sing out and dance round the room. She rushed to the mirror and gazed at the little white carving, nestling against her skin. So it really had happened…! And then, with a bat-like flutter, the jubilation was gone and she felt herself slipping back into a bad dream. Those horrible eyes in the font … that terrible mad laughter … would they try and get her back again…? Perhaps they wouldn't have enough crystal water … with any luck … but then … how would they manage without her – Uru and Jandus, Helio and the Master and the Dame? What would happen to them…? Sammie clapped her hands to her head to try and stop the sudden whirling of thoughts.

A floorboard creaked in the passage outside. She whisked off the sweater, leapt into bed in her T-shirt and pulled the covers up to her nose as a tangle of dark curls appeared and Mick's head slid slowly round the door. He glanced at the bed and the heap of discarded clothes on the floor. Then he sidled into the room and closed the door softly behind him.

"Where've you been?" he asked accusingly.

Sammie grunted in what she hoped was a sleepy-sounding way and turned over with her eyes still closed. But Mick was not to be fooled.

"Don't pretend. I heard you coming upstairs." He sat down heavily on one of Sammie's legs.

"Ow!" she said. "Get off! You're hurting me."

Mick made no effort to move. "Well…?"

"Well, what?" Sammie replied through clenched teeth.

"Well … where've you been?"

"Nowhere. I just went downstairs to get a drink."

"Must've been a long drink."

"Oh? And why's that?"

Mick slid off the bed and walked slowly over to the window. He poked his head between the curtains and said: "I never heard you going downstairs."

"You were probably asleep."

"No I wasn't."

"Well then, I tiptoed, didn't I."

"I don't believe you."

Sammie sat up. "Believe what you like. I went downstairs to get a drink. Anyway, did I invite you in here? It's six o'clock in the morning. Push off back to your own room."

Mick ignored her and remained at the window. "Whose footprints are those on the grass?"

Sammie said nothing.

Mick turned round, blinking behind his glasses.

"You've been to the wood, haven't you?"

Sammie sighed. "Yes, Mick, I've been to the wood."

He eyed her suspiciously. "What for?"

"Nothing special. I went for a walk. I woke up early and it was such a lovely morning I just felt like going to the wood. I watched the sunrise at the mere."

"I didn't think you knew the way to the mere," said Mick.

"Well, I found it, didn't I," Sammie replied.

Mick squinted at the pile on the floor. "Why are your clothes all damp?"

"Because I lay down on the grass to watch the sunrise and it was all dewy."

Mick's eyes narrowed. "Where?"

"Beside the mere, of course. For heaven's sake, Mick. Is this the Inquisition or something? I woke up early. I went for a walk. Now I'm back in bed again."

Mick said nothing.

"Look, I haven't done anything wrong. Even if I had it'd be none of your business. So just leave me alone, all right? You're really starting to bug me."

Once again Mick ignored her. He stood by the window, staring at her in chilly silence. For a moment she was reminded of the raven, stripping away her thoughts with its cruel black eyes...

"Please, Mick," she tried again, "just go back to..."

"And I suppose you found that by the mere?" Mick interrupted, pointing at the owl.

Sammie put her hands to her throat. She could feel a guilty flush flowing to her cheeks.

"Of … of course I didn't," she blustered.

"Well, I've never seen you wear it before," Mick said flatly. "Where did it come from?"

"One of my schoolfriends gave it to me."

Mick stared at her.

"I don't believe you just went for a walk. I don't believe you went to the mere. You couldn't have lain beside it because there's trees all the way round, right up to the boathouse. In fact, I don't believe a word you've said."

Now Sammie could feel the anger coming – as it always did. She took a deep breath, lay down and pulled the duvet up. "Well, that's your problem – because I'm telling the truth. So now you can just push off!" My version of the truth, anyway, she thought, turning away from him.

For a moment Mick was silent. Sammie held her breath, wondering whether he was going to lose his temper and jump on her – he'd done it before. Then she heard him say coldly:

"If you're hiding something from me, Sammie, I'll find out. Don't you worry. I'll find out, all right."

* * *

Sammie had forgotten it was Saturday. To her great relief, Mick's father had promised to take him fishing. They set off after breakfast, almost invisible beneath all their paraphernalia.

Sammie's mother sat down at the kitchen table and poured herself another cup of tea.

"Well, what about *our* project now?" she asked.

Strangely – because she usually remembered everything – Sammie's mind remained blank.

"What were we going to do?" she asked.

"Re-arrange the living room, of course!" replied her mother. "Surely you remember! We talked about where we were going to put everything... Anyway," she glanced out of the kitchen window, "d'you still want to help? You don't have to. It's such a lovely day."

"No, I'll help," said Sammie. It wasn't just that her brain didn't seem to be working this morning. There was something else – the unpleasant sensation of a bad dream still lingering on. It made her feel she wasn't properly connected to the world around her. Maybe it would help to be doing things.

They worked hard, moving the furniture about, dusting and cleaning, taking down the books, polishing ornaments. They chattered away, but Sammie found she was hardly taking in anything her mother said. Her mind kept flipping back to the valley and her hands strayed constantly to the little lump beneath the neck of her sweatshirt. Before coming down for breakfast she'd decided to take off the little fishbone carving, but somehow she hadn't been able to. It wasn't so much that her fingers couldn't undo the leather thong, more that they wouldn't. Now it was like a hole in a tooth. She couldn't stop touching it – even though each time she did, she wished it wasn't there.

"Time for elevenses!" announced her mother after they'd been working for an hour or so. She went to put the kettle on and Sammie sat down on the floor by a pile of old photograph albums. She took the top one and opened it in the middle.

Brighton 1936, it said at the top of the page. Beneath, were half a dozen faded black-and-white photographs of a family holiday. Mother, father and two daughters on the beach, riding donkeys with straw hats, sitting in an open-topped bus, eating ice-creams on the pier, making a huge sandcastle. And then one quite different from the others, that made the hairs stand up on the back of Sammie's neck.

One of the girls lay on her stomach on the bank of a little lake, gazing into the water. The lake was surrounded by trees. It was about the length of a tennis court, but shaped in a crescent, like an untidy new moon. Down one side stood a bed of reeds from which a coot had just paddled out…

Beneath the photo was written: E.L.'s Mystery Picture!

Sammie's hands felt clammy as her mother came back into the room and set down a tray. She glanced at the open album and exclaimed:

"Well, I never! Auntie Dot's old snapshots! Haven't looked at them for ages."

Sammie waited until the tea was poured and her mother was sitting down, then pointed to the photo and asked as calmly as she could:

"What was the mystery?"

Her mother laughed. "One of those weird stories – if you believed Auntie Dot! She was the only one that ever really talked about it, anyway."

"What happened?" asked Sammie impatiently.

"More what didn't happen really," her mother replied. "They were on holiday in Brighton. Auntie Dot was nine and her sister – my mother – your gran – was about your age. In the garden of their guest house was a pond with goldfish in it. According to Auntie Dot, Gran used to spend hours staring into the water. She was a bit of a dreamer."

She took a sip of tea and went on: "Now, their dad had a new camera. He was very proud of it and the girls weren't allowed near it – quite right too, I expect. Cameras were delicate things in those days, and expensive too. But Auntie Dot was a devil and one afternoon when her dad wasn't looking, she picked it up and sneaked a shot of Gran by the pond – that's what she said anyway, and Gran never denied it. Mind you, they could be thick as thieves, those two…"

"And…?" Sammie could sometimes strangle her mother for the way she spun out her stories.

"And – when they got home and had the film developed, everyone got a big surprise. Because, lo and behold, there was a photo that Great Grandad hadn't taken and didn't know anything about. And what's more – it wasn't the photo Auntie Dot thought she'd taken, either. Gran was in it all right, but she wasn't by a goldfish pond. Oh, no! She was by this lake that none of them had ever seen before in their lives – not Auntie Dot, not Great Grandad, not Great Grandma, not even Gran, or so she said at the time. And even if she was fibbing – even if she had been there, she couldn't have taken a photo of herself, could she? So how had it got there?"

Sammie shivered. "Gran was called Betty, wasn't she?" she asked.

Her mother nodded.

"So who's E.L?"

"Her," said her mother. "Gran. Elizabeth Leathwaite. Betty's short for Elizabeth."

"Of course!" Sammie replied. She could feel the goose-pimples all over her body. Elizabeth! Her own grandmother? Surely not! And yet it seemed too much to be a coincidence. The strange feeling she'd had, and the look Helio had given her, when they'd been going through that picture book... Could it really have been her own gran who'd been to the valley, the first Beyonder...?

"What was Gran like?" she asked, trying to sound normal.

Her mother smiled and shook her head. "Hard to describe really. We always got on pretty well. We loved each other, I s'pose. And drove each other mad. Like you and me! Like most mothers and daughters..." She paused, staring into the fireplace, then said: "I'll tell you one thing, though. She had what they call 'healing hands'. She could make things better just by putting her hands on them. I remember once or twice, when I'd taken a bump, she'd put her palms over the place and I'd feel like a tingling warmth coming out of them. It always took the pain right away."

Before Sammie could say anything, her mother went on:

"That reminds me – talking of unusual things – I had the weirdest dream about you last night. I forgot to tell you earlier, what with getting their sandwiches ready and all…"

"Oh?" said Sammie.

"Yes. You were in a boat on a big lake … you were with this little brown man and … wait a minute … there was a huge white bird somewhere … an owl maybe … yes, an owl … and it was sort of … looking after you…" Her mother paused and shook her head. "I've never been able to make head nor tail of dreams!"

It was all Sammie could do to keep the tremor from her voice as she said: "That was a nice thing to dream, wasn't it, Mum?"

Sammie's excitement didn't last for long. As the day wore on, the more she thought about the valley, the more uncomfortable she felt. And the more she tried not to think about it, the more she was left with a nasty, nagging sense of unfinished business.

The fishermen came home in the early evening, empty-handed as usual. They were still so busy discussing their day's adventures that they seemed hardly to notice when Sammie made an excuse soon after supper and went upstairs. It wasn't dark yet, but she climbed into bed, read for a few minutes and quickly fell asleep.

Her alarm clock told her it was three in the morning when she woke up again. She felt strangely restless. There were things scurrying about in her mind and she knew that she wouldn't get back to sleep easily. She put on the light and tried to read, but she couldn't concentrate. So she got out of bed and went quietly downstairs to make herself a mug of hot chocolate.

As soon as she entered the kitchen she saw the thin shaft of light coming from the fridge. Mick must've been down here, she thought. Mum would never have left it open.

She closed the fridge door and put on the main light, then went over to the cooker and reached up to the shelf beside it for the matches to light the gas ring. But the big box of kitchen matches wasn't there. And something else was missing too. After a few moments she realized it was the brass paraffin lamp they kept for emergencies. It usually sat on the shelf beside the matches.

She stood still, sensing that something was wrong. Then, almost before she knew what she was doing, she was tiptoeing back upstairs. She crept along the passage and stopped outside Mick's room. The door was shut.

Holding her breath, she put her hand on the handle and gently turned. The door swung open and she poked her head into the room. Her heart sank as she saw immediately that the bed was empty.

Mick had gone.

She stood in the doorway and stared into the darkened room. This has got something to do with what happened this morning, she thought. And if it has, then I suppose I'm partly responsible. Oh, drat him! What could he be up to?

For a moment it occurred to her to go and wake her mum and stepdad, but she quickly thought better of it. Something told her that her own early-morning exploit should stay a secret for the time being – and if Mick found himself in trouble, the first thing he'd do would be try and shift the blame on to her. No. She'd have to go and find him herself, before he did something really stupid – if he hadn't already. She'd start by checking the garden shed. If his bike was still there, then he wouldn't have gone far. If it wasn't... Well, she'd worry about that later.

She went into her bedroom and got dressed, then tiptoed downstairs again. She went outside, making her way gingerly towards the garden shed. It was pitch black inside and she groped ahead of her. There! That felt like a bicycle. She ran her fingers along the handlebars until they met the lamp. It was hers, she could tell by the shape. She switched it on and gave a sigh of relief to see that Mick's bike was there too. So he'd probably just gone to the wood or the mere. Well, that was something, at least.

Taking the lamp with her, she left the shed and crossed the stile. Within a few paces the trees had closed in around her. The lamp beam suddenly seemed terribly feeble, the darkness intense and menacing. Why on earth am I doing this? she thought with a shiver. And for a creep like Mick, of all people?

At that moment a glimmer caught her eye. She stopped and peered into the gloom. The glimmer vanished, then reappeared. It moved jerkily through the wood, as if whoever held it was unsure of what lay underfoot.

She switched off her own light and headed towards it as quietly as she could, tiptoeing over fallen branches and ignoring the brambles that scraped at her legs. When she was only a short distance away, the light stopped moving, just the other side of a large rhododendron bush. Sammie froze.

A minute passed and the light stayed still. Very slowly she got down on all fours and began to worm her way beneath the bush. She inched forwards until she was right at the very edge of the undergrowth. The light was almost above her head now, and still it didn't move. Sammie drew in her breath, bunched her muscles and stood up.

"Found you…" she began. But the words died on her lips as the light exploded into a fountain of brilliantly coloured jewels, sparkling amongst the shadowy trees and dancing over the still, dark water of the little lake which lay before her.

She took a pace towards the bank and a second explosion lit up the darkness beyond with a deep, fiery glow. The next instant the lights gathered themselves into a glittering spiral that spun down into the water in a beckoning, spangled whirlpool.

Unable to stop herself, she took another pace towards it, then another and then she was stepping off the bank and down into the brilliant light, down, down, down…

PART TWO

Chapter 11

Eggs for Breakfast

"Krrik-krrik."

A little black-faced gull was perched on a nearby rock.

"Krrik-krrik," it went again.

Sammie sat up and looked about. She was on a shingle beach with waves licking the pebbles at her feet. To left and right shimmered the sunlit lake. Ahead lay a scattering of little islands. All around, jagged, snow-capped mountains towered like dragon's teeth into a hazy sky...

Please let me be dreaming, she prayed. But no, she could feel the sun's warmth on her face, the hardness of the pebbles beneath her, and that strange tingling feeling inside, not so strong as before, but still quite unmistakable. Dream or reality – she suddenly wasn't sure she could tell the difference any longer – this was the valley.

She felt like screaming. What right had they to

pluck her from her safe, cosy life at Mere Cottages? What right had they to bring her back to their wretched valley with its mad Crystal Keeper and its creepy, unpredictable animals? And what made them think she'd lift a finger to help them?

But even before the questions had finished forming in her mind, she knew the answers. She was their only hope now. It was quite simple: Sammie – or some unimaginable catastrophe they were powerless to prevent. She had the nasty feeling that two-way spells had nothing to do with it any longer. Things had got beyond that point. The only way she was ever going to get home this time was to go and – well, do what they wanted her to do…

The gull hopped off its rock and took a couple of paces towards her. It stopped and cocked its head. Oh, no, she thought to herself with a shiver. And I've only been here a couple of minutes…

But the little bird didn't come any closer. Instead, it looked at her, then looked away again, lifting its beak as if to point towards the trees behind her. It did this several times, then turned and scurried towards the back of the beach, where it stopped again and glanced over its shoulder.

Sammie took a wary step towards it.

"Krrik-krrik," it went again, lifting into the air.

"Do you … want me to follow you?" she asked hesitantly.

The little gull nodded its head. She was beginning to think it actually looked rather friendly.

She took another step forward, then froze with dread as a familiar voice called out:

"Sammie! Wait, wait!"

She turned round. Panting along the shingle, frantically waving his arms, came Mick. He stopped in front of her, his face pale and his eyes wide with bewilderment.

"What in the *hell* are you doing here?" Sammie had never sworn before in her life, but this seemed like a good moment to start.

"I … I … d-don't know," Mick stammered. "Wh-where are we?"

Somewhere I certainly hoped I'd never see you, she thought. In his trainers and shorts, baggy T-shirt and back-to-front baseball cap, he looked so out of place she would have laughed if she hadn't felt like murdering him.

"I don't believe this! I just don't believe it! How dare you be here!" She was shouting, but she didn't care. "You want to know where we are, do you? I bet you do. Well, you can forget it, Mick. I'm not going to tell you anything. You wouldn't believe me

111

anyway." She paused to catch her breath. "You tell me how *you* got here. That's what I want to know. Go on!"

Mick hung his head and said nothing.

There was a funny smell about him, she noticed now. Something burnt. She looked again and saw that his eyebrows and the hair sticking out under the band of his baseball cap had gone brown and crinkly.

"Wait a minute…" She leant forward and sniffed. "You're all singed. What have you been doing?"

Still Mick said nothing.

She cast her mind back to the mere and for some reason found herself picturing the second, fiery explosion. Why…? And then it came to her. Of course! It had nothing to do with the Lights.

"You were up to something back there in the wood," she said. "You made something blow up, didn't you? Oh, boy, you're really going to be for it when we get back!"

It gave her some satisfaction to see him looking so sheepish.

"That's how you got here, isn't it," she went on, thinking out loud. "You set something off and it accidentally blew you in here with me." It was the only explanation she could think of. No one in their right mind would have brought him here on purpose. "Is that what happened, Mick?"

Mick scuffed his feet in the shingle.

Sammie shook her head in exasperation. What did I do to deserve this? she wondered.

"Krrik-krriiik!" The gull was beginning to sound impatient. It was standing on a nearby rock, hopping from one foot to another. Mick bent down and picked a pebble from the shingle. Before Sammie could stop him, he'd taken aim and hurled it. The little bird danced out of the way, chittering angrily.

"Oy!" yelled Sammie. "That's our guide. Don't you dare do that again!"

Mick reached at once for another pebble, but before he could throw it, Sammie grabbed his wrist and dug her nails in as hard as she could. He gave a startled squawk and the pebble dropped to the ground.

"I think we'd better get something straight," hissed Sammie furiously. "You're the last person in the world I wanted to see here – but I'm obviously stuck with you. So if you don't want me to abandon you, you'd better blinking well behave."

"What do I need you for?" muttered Mick. The sheepish look had gone and his usual scowl had returned. "I'll be fine."

"Don't be a twit, Mick," said Sammie. "You don't know where we are. *I* don't even know where we are right now. But I do know what's going on in this valley – and it's not funny, believe me. So if you want to stay in one piece, you do *exactly* what I tell you to from now on. Get it?"

Mick grunted something Sammie couldn't hear. She nodded to the little bird and it set off again. Furious though she was, she felt a spring in her step. It made a nice change to have the upper hand with her stepbrother. She could sense him plodding along sullenly at her heels.

Leaving the beach behind, they entered the shade of an oak wood. There was an unusually peaceful feeling about it. The trees stood apart from one another like solitary, sleepy old men. Birdsong rang through their branches and a huge scarlet butterfly drifted lazily in front of them. They had not gone far when the sound of a human voice began to drift towards them, echoing under the mantle of the wood. Sammie quickened her step and soon a glimpse of brilliant green indicated a clearing ahead. Not wishing to interrupt the voice, she stopped just short of the edge of the trees. Mick stopped a little behind her. They stood and listened:

114

I sit at my loom beneath the sun,
Watching the patterns I have spun
And the branches above of age untold
Dapple my thread in green and gold.

I flash my fingers and pedal my toes
As backwards and forwards the shuttle goes.
The threads pack tighter
As the colours grow brighter
And little by little my picture grows.

I am the Weaver and this is my song,
Singing it gladly all day long.
My life is the shuttle, sliding away,
Weaving its story day by day.

As the last notes of the song died away, Sammie could contain her curiosity no longer. She stepped into the clearing and stopped at once, struck with wonder at the scene that greeted her.

In the centre, directly ahead of her, stood an enormous and ancient oak tree. Its spreading canopy of leaves rustled and fluttered with the sound of a distant green waterfall. Beneath it, dappled with golden mosaics of sunlight, sat hundreds of animals and birds. The extraordinary sense of peacefulness was even stronger here, and she knew at once that no harm would come to her amongst these creatures. In any case, their backs were towards her and all were intent on the bent figure of a little old man with a mane of snow-white hair. He was perched on a high stool at a wooden loom, as big as a billiards table, wedged between two of the oak tree's massive roots.

Click-click, click-click went the shuttle as the old man's hands flew back and forth across the top of the loom. Below, his feet moved furiously up and down on a set of pedals.

All around him, shoulder-to-shoulder in bright-eyed rows, sat hares and rabbits, squirrels, mice of all kinds, shrews and voles by the score, all of them quite undismayed by the company of three foxes and a small tribe of weasels. A clan of raccoons surrounded an old badger who had fallen asleep and toppled sideways off his haunches. A nanny goat and her kid sat together, chewing thoughtfully. From beneath an enormous wild sow poked a row of little black snouts. In a small clearing amongst the otherwise jam-packed congregation sat a porcupine, attended by two hedgehogs.

And everywhere, perched on backs, shoulders and even tails, were the birds: robins and wrens, bullfinches and bluetits, pigeons, plovers and partridges, ducks and divers, hawks and hens, wagtails and waders, geese and a swan and even a great black buzzard standing sound asleep on one corner of the loom.

Sammie felt as if she could stand for ever on the threshold of this enchanted circle. But something told her that it was time she introduced herself. "You stay just here!" she whispered fiercely to Mick. Then she stepped into the open and coughed politely.

For a moment there was a deafening silence as the loom ceased its clicking and a thousand pairs of eyes turned slowly in her direction. Then the Weaver's face broke into a broad, wrinkled grin.

He hopped down from his stool, shooing the animals and birds out of his way, and bustled towards her. His head bobbed up and down within its halo of white hair and a much-mended red cloak rippled around his shoulders.

As he stopped in front of her, Sammie found herself looking into the oldest face she had ever seen. It was wrinkled and gnarled, like the bark of the oak tree, and yet sunk within it, beneath a pair of bushy white eyebrows, were the eyes of a mischievous child. They were like two shiny brown pools, the colour of peat-water and bright as new pennies. They beamed at her impishly as their owner held out a bony hand and exclaimed:

117

"A visitor to Oak Holm! My word! You must be Sammie! I expect you'd like some breakfast."

Before Sammie had time to reply the old man turned round and clapped his hands.

"Come now. I know we don't often have visitors, but haven't I told you it's rude to stare?"

A thousand pairs of eyes were lowered.

"That's better. Now, this is Sammie. She's come a long way to see us – well, me actually – and she has no time to waste. So be off with you! No more weaving today."

The audience began to wander off into the wood, grunting, squeaking, snuffling and twittering.

"They're my assistants, you see," he explained to Sammie. "They help me when I'm weaving."

"How do they do that?" she asked.

A fond smile tugged at his wrinkles as he replied: "At my age I need all the encouragement they can give me. So, they will me to weave. Also, they … how can I put it … they lend their hearts and their minds. You see, my friends hear and see and feel things quite differently. And for my story to be complete it must contain the wisdom of the animal kingdom as well."

Sammie wasn't quite sure what he was talking about, but she nodded anyway.

Now only the gull remained, hovering just behind her.

"Ah, Krrik!" said the Weaver. The little bird fluttered down on to his shoulder. He reached up and stroked its head. "Thank you for bringing my guest…"

"Er – guests, I'm afraid…" said Sammie, who had been waiting for the right moment to break this awkward piece of news. She glanced at where she'd left Mick, waiting at the edge of the clearing. But there was no sign of him.

"Oh, no!" she mumbled in horror. "Oh, drat it!"

"Guests, did you say?" inquired the Weaver. He seemed not to have grasped this new turn of events.

"Um – I – er – thought so," said Sammie, blushing.

"Who?" asked the Weaver.

There seemed little point pretending, so Sammie told him exactly what had happened. "And now he's gone and disappeared," she concluded, "stupid idiot that he is."

The Weaver didn't seem the least worried. "Oh, never mind," he said cheerfully, curling a lock of hair between his fingers and sticking it into his ear. "He can't come to any harm here."

"Are you sure?" asked Sammie anxiously.

"Quite sure!" said the old man. "Let him wander about if he wants to. We'll find him when we need him." He turned to Krrik, still perched on his shoulder, and whispered something. Then he said: "Now off you go, and keep watch well. We want no interruptions."

The little bird nodded and flew off.

"What's he keeping watch for?" asked Sammie, following the Weaver towards the huge tree.

"Why, spies of course," the old man replied as if it were the most obvious thing in the world.

"What sort of spies?" asked Sammie, alarmed.

"*His* spies – that madman in the forest – birds, fish, even butterflies. Anything that can get to Oak Holm. Oh, but don't you worry, my dear," the Weaver's eyes twinkled, "we spot them the minute they set foot here and send them packing."

"But what about your … er … assistants?"

"Humph! He can't touch *them*. Not so long as I'm here," exclaimed the old man scornfully. "Don't know why he bothers!"

Now they'd reached the foot of the tree. The Weaver scrambled over a tangle of huge roots and disappeared into a hole in the trunk. Sammie followed and found herself climbing steps which spiralled upwards inside the hollow tree. Eventually she popped up through an opening in the floor of a little room.

It was a fraction smaller than her bedroom at home, but so much darker and so incredibly cluttered with books, candle stubs, unwashed wooden platters and spare bits of loom, that it seemed only half the size. The only light came from one grimy pane of glass that had been jammed into a hole where a branch had once grown. The walls were speckled with knots and whorls and there was a musty, woody smell.

"Well now," said the old man as she stood up, "what would you like for breakfast? I've got oak-apples, wild mushrooms, beechnuts, chestnuts, blackberries ... I think there's even some nettle and harebell soup left over..."

He caught the look on Sammie's face and gazed at her intently for a moment, then shook his head.

"Hmmm. Silly of me. Not Beyonder food, eh? Need something a bit more toothsome, a bit more filling..." He scratched his head for a moment, then a grin spread amongst the wrinkles. "I have it! An egg! You'd like an egg! Well?"

"That would be ... fine," said Sammie, wondering what kind of egg he might produce.

"Splendid!" said the Weaver. He bustled over to an armchair and vanished behind it. There was an outburst of indignant clucking and a large red hen scuttled out. The old man followed a moment later, bearing two speckled brown eggs.

"There!" he announced, beaming. "Two hen's eggs. Now you sit down while I get things ready." He waved her to a small table with two stools.

"How did you know I was coming?" Sammie asked as the old man shoved twigs into a little black pot-bellied stove and puffed away at them. The room began to fill with smoke.

"Uru came to see me, earlier this morning," he replied, coughing and spluttering. "He was on his way to the forest to create a diversion – distract the madman so that he wouldn't cause trouble while they tried to get you back."

"And how did they get me back?" asked Sammie.

"Usual way," said the Weaver matter-of-factly. "Crystal water. Very last drop they had."

"And was it … the um … normal … I mean … two–way spell?" she asked, despite herself.

The Weaver shrugged. "Wouldn't know. Don't have anything to do with spells, myself. That's the Dame's business. Anyway, she managed it, even though it nearly killed her this time – so Uru said. And she landed you right here, where they wanted you."

"I bet they didn't bargain on two of us," said Sammie.

The Weaver shrugged. "Makes no difference. *You're* here. That's what counts."

But they don't know what a liability Mick can be, thought Sammie. We've only been here an hour and already he's gone and vanished.

"So what happens now?" she asked.

"The Master's sending a ship. It'll pick you up later on and take you across the lake. Uru'll meet you and put you on your way."

That was good news, at least, thought Sammie. It would be lovely to see the owl again.

"Put me on my way to where?" she asked without thinking.

"To the forest. To the Crystal Sanctuary, of course," the Weaver replied, placing a saucepan on the stove.

"Of course," said Sammie in a small voice. She changed the subject quickly. "How is Uru?"

"Tired, I'd say," said the Weaver. "And no wonder! Chasing all over the valley every day, and all because of that … that lunatic! Tut-tut! A nice mess we've got ourselves into!"

That was putting it mildly, thought Sammie with a shiver. Then she remembered what Helio had said about the old man. "If anyone knows what to do, he will." She must have been brought to Oak Holm so that he could help her. It was a cheering thought. Well, she'd find out soon enough…

A few minutes later the Weaver bustled over with four pieces of toast and two brown eggs sitting side by side in a double eggcup. Sammie set to ravenously. The Weaver watched her in silence while she ate. Then, when every last morsel was gone, he rocked back on his stool, folded his arms and asked pleasantly:

"And why have you come to see me?"

Sammie was taken aback. She looked hard at the old man but his face gave nothing away. The brown eyes still twinkled and a smile played around his lips.

"Don't … don't you know?" she stammered.

"Yes, yes," replied the Weaver. "*I* know. Of course I know. But I want to find out whether *you* know."

Sammie thought hard. "Well … I think you're going to help me…"

"Hmmmm," replied the Weaver slowly. "But with what?"

She didn't want to have to say it, but there was something in the old man's gaze that seemed to drag it out of her.

"Curing the Crystal Keeper," she said.

He gave a little snort. "Now whatever makes you think I can help you with a thing like that?"

"Because you're the Weaver, of course," replied Sammie, starting to feel annoyed. "And Helio and the Dame said you're the wisest person in the whole valley."

"Oh, I am. Indeed I am. But cure the Crystal Keeper? Goodness me, if I knew how to do that I'd have gone and done it myself long ago."

"Then what on earth am I doing here?" she asked crossly. "How *can* you help me?"

At this the Weaver rocked forward again on his stool and clapped his hands in delight. The bushy eyebrows wriggled like a pair of caterpillars as he exclaimed:

"Famous! Famous! That's the question! Now we're where we ought to be! Now we can start!"

Sammie looked at him in bewilderment as he fumbled excitedly for a lock of hair and wound it around his ear. But before she had time to say anything, he continued:

"You see, Sammie, the way I can help you isn't necessarily the way you thought." He wagged his finger at her. "And there's a lesson already! If you expect too much, you can end up getting nasty surprises."

"You can get them even when you're not expecting anything," said Sammie with feeling.

The Weaver nodded sympathetically. "Yes, of course. Your – er – companion. But no need to worry about him at the moment. He's perfectly all right. Anyway – back to the important business. Now, what matters most in the world is that people do the things they're supposed to, to the very best of their ability. So, a Master rules the valley, a fisherman casts his nets on the lake, and Sammie cures the Crystal Keeper. I can't teach them how to do these things because I don't know how myself. But if they want to do the very best job they can, I can show them where they'll find what they need. I can help them to look inside themselves, Sammie."

The Weaver leant across the table and took Sammie's hands in his. His wrinkles creased into a brilliant smile and his eyes twinkled impishly.

"You may think my teaching a little peculiar," he said, "but I promise you it works. Now, if you're ready...?"

He rose from the table and vanished through the hole in the floor. Sammie followed him.

Chapter 12

The Lesson

"Here you are," announced the Weaver. He stopped by the loom and pointed to it. "Your lesson!"

Sammie felt more confused than ever. She went closer and found herself gazing down at an immense, unfinished weaving, glowing in the dappled sunlight.

"Is that what you want me to learn?" she asked anxiously. "How to weave?"

"Good gracious me, no!" exclaimed the Weaver with a chuckle. "Your lesson is much simpler. All you need do is look at my life's work. In fact you can start this minute." He peered up at the sun. "I'll be back in an hour, at midday, to see what you've learned."

Leaving Sammie to the loom, he set off across the clearing with his white hair bobbing and his shabby red cloak flapping.

Sammie clambered on to the stool and allowed her eye to roam the magnificent pageant until it came to

127

rest on a scene no bigger than the palm of her hand. A great white owl and a little ragged blonde girl were climbing down a mountainside in the pale light of dawn.

She gasped with pride and delight. Tiny as they were, the figures were perfect in every detail.

Other images began to catch her eye: a tall, elegant Crystal Keeper standing by the marble stone at the edge of the forest; a Dame bent over the font with the Lights sparkling like a rainbow above her; two great ships on the lake...

Soon she forgot about everything else as the images drew her in and she began to realize that it was the weaving itself that was leading her from one scene to the next, deliberately shaping her journey through this fabulous landscape.

Every tale ever told was here, it seemed. There were battles and banquets, marriages and masquerades, plots and pilgrimages, chivalry and treachery, feast and famine, music and magic. And it was not only the human story of the valley that the weaving unfolded. Journeys and homecomings, snowstorms and whirlwinds, mountain eyries, forest lairs, floods, fires and fights to the death – the kingdom of nature had its place too, as the Weaver had said.

The longer Sammie looked, the more she felt she

was seeing the images not just with her eyes but also with her heart. She felt herself becoming flooded with a great warmth. And still the weaving led her on.

There was a loud Ahem! behind her. She turned round to find the old man standing at her shoulder.

"You weren't away for very long," Sammie remarked. It seemed like only a few minutes.

"Midday precisely!" he said, squinting up at the sun again. "Now, come and sit with me in the sunshine and we'll find out whether an old man's weaving has done its work."

Feeling a little dizzy, Sammie climbed down from the stool and followed him out from beneath the tree. They sat down together on the grass.

"Now tell me," he said, "did you enjoy your lesson?"

"Oh, yes! It was wonderful," she replied, glancing back at the loom. "I've never seen anything like that before."

"And what do you think you learned?"

"I'm not sure I could really tell you," she answered, anxiously but truthfully.

To her surprise, the old man looked pleased.

"Splendid!" he said. "Too much thinking does you no good, no good at all. Now, forget your brain and tell me what you feel."

Sammie hesitated for a moment, feeling a little embarrassed. But his eyes twinkled encouragement and she explained:

"I'm glowing all through. I feel really warm inside. It's sort of as if my heart's – well, getting bigger, I s'pose. That's the only way I can describe it."

Her answer seemed to excite the Weaver. He rubbed his hands together and leant closer to her.

"And what would you call this feeling?"

"It's definitely a good feeling," replied Sammie, thinking out loud. "It's like what I felt when I was with Uru, or sometimes with Mum, or when I've done something for someone I like and they're really pleased about it … I suppose you'd call it – love…"

Now the Weaver's eyes were positively sparkling.

"And what is the most important thing in the world?" he asked.

At once, images from the weaving tumbled into her mind and as they flickered past she felt the inner glow intensify. A prince's love for his princess, a mother's love for her children, a warrior's love for his companions. The love of a farmer for his land, a healer for the sick, even a hunter for his prey. In all its different guises it was love that accounted for the happiness in the world, love that inspired people to do the best for themselves and others.

"Love…?" Sammie replied.

"Love!" exclaimed the old man. "Capital!" He clapped his hands delightedly. Then he fell serious and said:

"But loving isn't always easy, you know. The hardest of all is to love someone you dislike or disagree with. Someone who frightens you or who you find disgusting. Someone who tricks you or takes advantage of you. And sometimes we need to be able to find that love."

The Weaver paused and looked Sammie directly in the eye. "Can you, Sammie? Can you find that love when you need it?"

"I don't know," Sammie answered. Why was it that he kept making her think of Mick? "I suppose I can try," she added doubtfully.

"That's enough," said the old man with a fond smile. "You have learned well. All any of us can do is try."

There was a commotion in the trees behind them. Sammie turned round to see Mick making his way through the wood, surrounded by a flock of honking, waddling white geese. She couldn't tell whether they were simply showing him the way, or driving him along like a lost sheep. And from the startled expression on his face, it looked as if Mick wasn't sure either.

"Aha," said the Weaver with a grin. "Our other guest. And right on time, too!"

The geese stopped at the edge of the trees, leaving Mick to make his way into the clearing. Sammie got to her feet, thinking she'd better make the introductions. Now she could see that Mick's mouth and chin were stained almost black, as if he'd been feasting on berries or currants.

"Mick," she said as he stopped in front of them, "this is the – er – Mr – er – Weaver."

"I know," grunted Mick.

"Yes, yes!" said the Weaver cheerfully. "We've already met. Did you enjoy your breakfast, young man?"

"Yuh," said Mick.

"And my friends," he pointed to the geese, "they looked after you well?"

"Yuh," said Mick again.

The Weaver turned to Sammie. "You see, we happened to bump into each other while you were busy," he gave her a tiny wink, "and we had the pleasantest chat! I was able to show Mick the best bramble patch on the whole of Oak Holm. And I asked the geese to stay and keep him company."

Keep an eye on him, you mean, thought Sammie.

At that moment there was a fluttering as Krrik landed on the Weaver's shoulder and put his beak to the old man's ear.

"Well, well!" he exclaimed. "More visitors. My, what a day!"

The little gull flew off again and they followed it through the trees to a small bay on the far side of the island. There, looking splendid in the sunlight with her emerald sail and her tall mast reaching for the sky, lay one of the ships Sammie had seen in the harbour. Now she could see the name, painted across the stern in gold letters: *Spirit of the Valley*. A rowing boat was making its way in to the shore.

They stepped down on to the beach and a few moments later there was a scrunch of shingle as the little boat rode the shallows. A sailor in a short white tunic climbed out and stood at the bows. The Weaver went ahead and spoke briefly to him, then beckoned to Sammie and Mick.

"Well," he said with a smile, "it's time for you to be on your way. I've explained to this good fellow here that there are two of you now. He'll tell the captain." He looked directly at Mick. "Well young man, take care of Sammie for us."

Mick blushed and mumbled something. The

Weaver turned to Sammie and gave a little cough:

"And you, young lady. Great deeds await you. So be off now, and remember your lesson!" His voice was matter-of-fact, but the twinkling brown eyes were moist and full of tenderness.

"I will," said Sammie. She looked at the little old man with his mane of white hair and faded red cloak, and wondered whether to give him a hug. It didn't seem quite right, so she reached for his wrinkled, bony hand and shook it.

"Thank you," she said, "thank you for helping me." Then she turned and followed Mick into the rowing boat.

As they pulled away from the shore the Weaver cupped his hands and shouted something. His voice was frail across the water, but Sammie thought he said:

"We'll be with you!"

Chapter 13

Overboard

There was a tense atmosphere on board *Spirit of the Valley*. Despite all the hustle and bustle of departure, Sammie noticed it at once. Something in the crew's faces told her that this was no ordinary voyage. She heard a soft whistle from Mick and turned to see him eyeing an armoury of glinting cutlasses and pikes stacked around the mast.

They followed the sailor across the deck, down a narrow stairway, along a passage, and into a little cabin. There were clothes here for Sammie, he said, and once he'd reported to the captain, he would bring something for Mick too.

As the door closed, Mick walked across to the porthole and stood there, staring out in thoughtful silence. Sammie looked at the white cotton robe, the soft suede boots and the woollen travelling cloak laid out on the bunk. She sat down and took off her jeans and sweatshirt, then picked up the robe and pulled it over her head. The cotton felt loose and cool against her skin.

She was tugging on the second boot when Mick turned back from the porthole. For a moment she was reminded of the way he'd stood at her bedroom window that morning when she'd first returned from the mere. But this time it wasn't accusation in his look. It was something which might have been envy, or a hint of grudging admiration – she couldn't tell which.

"I know why you're here," he said. "The Weaver told me."

"Well, you did say you'd find out what I was up to!" Sammie replied.

Mick ignored the joke and went on: "You're here to save them, aren't you."

"So everyone keeps telling me," said Sammie with a sigh. "Did he mention that I haven't the faintest idea how?"

Mick blinked. "No. But he – um – did say – er – that it's lucky I'm here too."

"Oh, he did, did he?" said Sammie. "And why's that?"

"Because I can help you. Because it'll be easier for us to do it together than for you to do it alone."

"Did he happen to tell you what 'it' is?" she asked.

Mick nodded.

"And how d'you think you'll help me with that?"

"I dunno. But I do want to help you, Sammie. Honestly. I know you don't want me along – but I'm here – and I could be really useful – in all sorts of ways. If you'll let me. The old man said so."

Sammie doubted it. It was much more likely that the Weaver had told him not to get in the way.

"This isn't some stupid game, you know," she said. "This is serious, Mick. Deadly serious. We might even be killed – or end up stuck here for ever."

"I know," said Mick. There was an eagerness in his look that she hadn't seen before, and something told her to beware of it…

The door gave a creak and opened a little. Sammie found herself looking into a pair of deep blue eyes. One of them winked.

"Helio!" she cried delightedly. "What on earth are you doing here?"

"Shhh!" Helio put a finger to his lips and stepped inside. He was grinning from ear to ear. Then he caught sight of Mick and a look of surprise crossed his face. "And who's this?" he asked.

"This is Mick – my stepbrother. Mick – this is Helio, the Master's son."

Helio held out his hand and said politely: "How

d'you do, Mick."

"Hello," grunted Mick. He shook Helio's hand but avoided his eye. The eagerness had suddenly gone.

Helio glanced at Sammie and raised an eyebrow.

"Mick came with me by accident," she explained. "And now he's here he's going to help. Anyway," she changed the subject quickly, "how did *you* get here? What's going on? How're the Master and Dame?"

Helio sat down on the bunk. His dark hair was its usual tangle. The deep blue eyes still held their wicked glint. But his tunic was crisp and clean and from a fine leather belt at his waist hung a sheathed dagger, its hilt glittering with precious stones. There was something different about him – a new sense of purpose maybe, thought Sammie. It came almost as a relief to see him grin again and hear him say:

"I shouldn't really be here at all – but I stowed away. I knew they were coming to pick you up at Oak Holm and I wanted to see you!"

"Oh, Helio! How did you do it?"

"Easy – I dressed up as a porter and came on board early this morning when they were loading provisions. Then I hid in the cabin next door."

"But what about your father and mother – surely they'll guess where you've gone," Sammie said. Mick appeared to be examining a picture on the cabin wall.

He had his back to them, but she could tell he was soaking up every word.

"Yes, I expect they will," Helio replied. "But they won't be able to do anything about it." He grinned again. "Uru's the only one who could catch up with *Spirit of the Valley* – and he's in the forest at the moment."

"But we're supposed to be meeting him, aren't we? That's what the Weaver said. This evening…"

"Yes. But it'll be too late by then. Uru can't take me back and the ship's got other things to do. So it looks as if you're stuck with me… You don't mind, do you?"

Sammie felt like hugging him. "Mind?" she said. "It's absolutely brilliant! Oh, Helio, I'm so pleased to see you."

"Me too," said Helio with a huge smile. "It seems like age…"

Mick spun round with a black look. "It's getting a bit crowded down here," he said. "Think I'll go on deck and get some air. Leave you two to it…"

Sammie's heart sank. "But – but you haven't got your clothes…"

Mick ignored her. He brushed past Helio, flung open the door and strode loudly away down the passage.

Helio turned to Sammie with a bewildered look. "Did I say something wrong?"

Sammie shook her head wearily. "He's impossible – that's all. I just wish he wasn't here." She sat down on the bunk beside Helio and told him what had happened. "So we're stuck with him," she ended with a sigh. "Anyway, tell me what's going on here. Why does everyone look so serious? What are all those weapons for?" She waved at the deck above her head.

Helio stared at his hands for a moment, then looked up seriously.

"Things have got pretty bad, Sammie. But you know that anyway, don't you? You wouldn't be here otherwise…" He shook his head. "So, where to begin…? Well, soon after you'd gone, more and more people began to disappear. Especially from the forest. We discovered that he was taking them to the Crystal Sanctuary and turning them into slaves – making them do whatever he wanted. Anyone who resisted, he sent to World's Edge."

"What's that?" asked Sammie.

"A huge cavern, right up in the top of the mountains. It looks out on the other side – beyond the valley. We know it as the place where the crystal's power ends. But the people who lived here before us – hundreds of years ago – they used World's Edge as

140

a refuge in times of danger. They carved a passage out of the rock – it goes up for miles through the heart of the mountains. You can get to it from the Crystal Sanctuary…"

"So he's locking people up there?" said Sammie.

Helio nodded. "Probably starving them as well. It's what he's been trying to do to us."

"What do you mean?" asked Sammie.

"You remember my father saying the harvest had failed?"

"Yes."

"Well, that was just the start of it. Since then, he's poisoned the orchards and meadows so all our fruit's gone and there's hardly any grass for the animals to eat. He's done something to the lake, too. The fish are dying. The poor fishermen are desperate."

Sammie shook her head in dismay.

"But I'm afraid even that's not all," Helio went on. "You see, Uru's just found out that he's started to gather his own army."

"What sort of an army?" asked Sammie in horror.

"Marsh things," Helio replied. "Beyond the mountains at the far end of the valley there's an enormous area of marshes. It's an awful place, full of swamps and quicksands. No one lives there, just insects and lizards and sawbacks…"

141

"Sawbacks?"

"Huge scaly things that lie in the water like sunken logs," Helio explained. "They've got a ridge, like sawteeth, down their backs. They're incredibly fierce and very strong."

Sammie shuddered.

"Anyway," he went on, "the Crystal Keeper's made all these horrible things speak and think and walk on their hind legs, and now they're gathering at the far end of the gorge. That's the steep, narrow place where the lake runs out between the mountains. It's the only way into or out of the valley. In the past, of course, the crystal stopped anything coming through that shouldn't have. But now..."

Sammie nodded.

"So, once *Spirit of the Valley* has put you – I mean us – ashore, she's going to head straight for the end of the lake. Her sister ship, *Heart of the Valley*, is following. Together, they're carrying about a hundred and fifty men. That's who the weapons are for. They're going to try and defend the gorge..."

Helio stopped speaking and looked down, as if he knew already that the expedition was doomed.

This was worse than anything she could have imagined, thought Sammie. In the brooding silence, the little cabin suddenly seemed close and airless.

"I think I need to get out of here," she said.

Helio nodded. "Shall I come with you?"

"Yes please," said Sammie. Then she hesitated. "But – what about – being a stowaway?"

Helio shrugged. "They can't really do anything. They might as well know."

"If Mick hasn't told them already," said Sammie.

Helio opened the door for her. They left the little cabin and went up on deck.

Spirit of the Valley was cutting a brisk pace across the sunlit water, her great emerald sail swollen with a warm breeze. Gulls wheeled overhead, dazzlingly white against the deep blue of the sky. All around the deck a brass rail glinted as it rose and fell gently against the distant shore. But talking to Helio seemed to have unlocked all Sammie's worst fears and misgivings. Now they weighed down on her like a leaden cloud that no view, however glorious, could lift.

At the stern, watching intently while a sailor did something with a piece of rope and a spike, stood Mick. He must have found somewhere else to change for now he was wearing a short white tunic and would have looked like everyone else on board were it not for the spectacles and back-to-front baseball cap. As it was, he looked utterly absurd, thought Sammie.

He glanced up and glared as they walked towards him.

"Go away!" he said.

"Mick, please…" said Sammie.

"Please yourself. You were right. You don't need me. Not with your boyfriend here."

"Oh, for goodness' sake, Mick! Don't be pathetic!"

"Well, what is he?" demanded Mick.

"He's not my boyfriend, anyway," said Sammie.

"What's boyfriend?" asked Helio, looking bewildered.

"Nothing – he's just being…" Sammie stopped as the sailor snapped sharply to attention and footsteps approached across the deck. She turned round to see a pleasant-looking man with a small golden badge pinned to his tunic.

"Pardon me for interrupting, but I'm your captain," he said with a polite smile, "and I'm very pleased to have you aboard, Sammie – if I may call you that?"

"Of course," said Sammie as he took her hand and gave a little bow.

Then he turned to Helio. "Welcome to you too, Mick."

"He's not Mick," came a disgruntled voice. "I am." Mick stepped out from behind Sammie and Helio.

144

"Oh!" said the captain in confusion. He looked at Mick, then Helio, then Mick again, nodding as he took in the spectacles and baseball cap. "I thought … well, no matter … please accept my apologies, Mick – and welcome."

There was a grunt from Mick and the captain turned back to Helio. "So who might you be, young man?"

Helio thrust out his hand and flashed a winning smile. "Helio, the Master's son – at your service, sir!"

This time the captain was caught completely off guard. Sammie felt quite sorry for him as his pleasant face creased in further confusion.

"But … but … I was not told…"

"Of course not," declared Helio, still smiling. "You see, I'm a stowaway."

"A stowaway," said the captain to himself, slowly digesting this startling piece of information. He looked again at Helio. "Well now, and what am I to do with a stowaway?"

But the question went unanswered for at that moment a sailor hurried up with a worried expression. He pointed down the lake to where something dark and spindly and sinister-looking was moving towards them across the water.

"What is it?" asked Sammie nervously.

The captain stared at it for some time before replying: "It looks like a waterspout. Yes, a waterspout, by the Lights! In all my years on the lake I've never seen one."

"It doesn't look very big," said Mick.

"That's because it's still far off," explained the captain. "But they *are* big – and very powerful too. And they move a lot quicker than we can."

"Oh," said Mick, as if he wished he hadn't mentioned it.

"So what do we do?" asked Helio.

"Pray to the Lights that it passes us by, or try and sail out of its way," he said gravely. "Now, with your leave, I must give orders."

The worried captain strode off and started issuing commands to the crew. Mick took off his baseball cap and began to fiddle with it nervously as Sammie and Helio exchanged grim glances, neither daring to voice what was in the other's mind: this is no coincidence.

The waterspout, meanwhile, continued to spin towards them and soon a dull rumble began to carry across the sunlit waters of the lake. *Spirit of the Valley* fled like a hunted deer as the captain barked orders, the helmsman spun the wheel, and the crew rushed to gather or slacken the great sails. But the waterspout followed relentlessly. No matter how swiftly they sped through the water, no matter how nimbly they changed course, the waterspout shadowed their every turn. Little by little it began to close in on them.

Unable to do anything else, Sammie, Helio and Mick stood at the stern, their argument quite forgotten, and watched in horror. It was as if they were defenceless animals, hypnotized by some great snake. For there was something truly snakelike about it as it reared up out of the lake and towered into the clear blue sky. The immense column swayed from side to side as it spun towards them, rippling continuously from its roots to its dark spreading crest which loomed like a cobra's hood against the heavens.

As it drew nearer, the sound grew louder and louder until the very timbers of the ship seemed to quiver. The waterspout was shrieking and moaning and roaring from the black depths of its tortured soul, drowning all other sound as it hungrily sucked in the air around it and gulped up the waters of the lake. The noise made Sammie's blood run cold and she put her hands to her ears, unable to stand it any longer. But still she couldn't look away.

Now the giant pillar of water was almost upon

them. She could see the boiling, foaming waters at its base where the wind around it had whipped the lake into a frenzy. She could also see that it was as wide as the ship and its great rippling wall of dark water reached so high it was starting to blot out the sun.

Then, all of a sudden, the air around her went dead. The great sail fell limp and it seemed as if *Spirit of the Valley* had stopped moving. Sammie tore her gaze away and for a long moment found herself staring across the deck to where the captain and crew stood frozen at their posts, their eyes fixed helplessly on the waterspout. Then an almighty blast of wind knocked her to the ground. A split second later darkness fell, the din rose to a crescendo and the waterspout struck.

So this is how it all ends, Sammie thought, as she was flung across the violently tilting deck and smacked into the woodwork again. Half winded and blinded by spray she reached out and groped for something to hang on to. Her hand eventually found the brass rail and she clung to it, waiting for the churning water that would surely crash down on her from out of the howling, raging darkness. Now *Spirit of the Valley* was bucking and twisting like a wounded animal. Through the roaring of the water-spout she could hear the agonized rending of wood and metal as the giant column of water smashed its way through the heart of the ship. But the crushing weight of water did not come.

Instead, there was a savage shriek as the wind curled around the stern and plucked Sammie from the desk as if she were a scrap of paper. She felt the air being sucked from her lungs, and wind-driven needles of spray flaying her skin, as she was drawn up and up into the roaring darkness and then flung far out over the side of the ship to tumble headlong into the boiling waters of the lake.

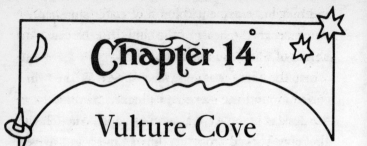

Chapter 14

Vulture Cove

She was dead. She had to be. She'd drowned and now she was in heaven or somewhere and she never did cure the Crystal Keeper. Oh, well, it didn't really matter... Nothing really mattered... She felt as if she no longer weighed anything. There was a soft light outside her eyelids. What would be the first thing she saw? Angels with harps? Fat pink cherubs?

Sammie opened her eyes and blinked in confusion. This didn't look like heaven.

It was sunset and she was lying half-in, half-out of the water. She'd come to rest on a sandbank near the shore of the lake, it seemed. Ahead was a cove, ringed by towering cliffs. At her side floated the remains of a wooden chair. There was no other sign of life to be seen.

She began to heave herself out of the water and suddenly she caught a whiff of the foulest stench she had ever smelt. I've got to be alive, she thought.

Nothing in heaven could possibly smell that bad. She stood up and stumbled on wobbly legs through the shallows. She'd gone only a short way when she saw where the horrible smell was coming from.

The waterline was littered with the bodies of hundreds of fish. They were bloated from the heat of the day, their dead eyes clouded, empty jaws gaping at the clouds of flies that buzzed greedily about the unexpected banquet.

Sammie held her nose tight shut as she stepped gingerly over the jumbled bodies. She made her way to the very back of the cove, as far from the fish as possible, and sank down against the cliff, wondering where on earth she was and how she'd got here. For a long time her brain simply wouldn't work. She sat and stared at the beach in front of her. Then, gradually, the events of the afternoon began to come back to her.

She felt a cold sweat break out as she relived the terrible last moment of *Spirit of the Valley*. Her stomach turned cartwheels as she remembered being plucked from the deck and hurled through the darkness into the water and then … the chair. Of course! It had crashed into the waves at her side as she'd struggled to the surface. She'd grabbed hold of it and somehow managed to hook her robe over it. It must have remained afloat, drifting in the currents, long after she'd passed out from exhaustion. And eventually she'd been washed up here.

But what about everyone else? The lake was calm and still as far as the eye could see. There was no sign of wreckage, no people in the water, nothing... Despair filled her as she thought of Helio and Mick, the captain and crew. Could they all have drowned? Her shoulders began to shake as salty tears streamed down her cheeks. And even if they'd survived, she'd never see them again because she was trapped here. She had no boat and she'd never climb the cliffs – they were far too high. So unless someone came to rescue her, she'd starve to death. I wish I'd drowned too, she thought wretchedly.

She sat and sobbed for a long time before something suddenly made her think of Uru. There was no reason why he shouldn't still come to her rescue! He must know about the sinking of *Spirit of the Valley* by now. She gazed across the lake and prayed aloud:

"Dear Uru, please, please hear me, wherever you are. Please come and take me away from this awful place. You found me before and I know you will this time."

But Uru did not come. The shadows lengthened. Dusk fell. And as dusk turned to darkness and still there was no sign of him, her hope faded and the despair returned. With no tears left to weep, she lay down on the sand at the base of the looming, shadowy cliffs, and fell into an exhausted sleep.

As the sun crept up over the lake there was a swish of wings and something landed on the sand.

"Uru!" cried Sammie, instantly awake.

But it wasn't Uru. It was a great black mountain-vulture, almost as tall as Sammie. It stood at the water's edge, looking at her unblinkingly with a mean little eye. It's wondering whether I'm worth eating, she thought with a shudder. But after a while it became clear that she wasn't as appealing to the horrible creature as the fish.

Still not daring to move, Sammie watched in disgust as the scavenger poked around amongst the carcascs with its great hooked beak. Then, with a snakelike movement of its featherless, pink neck, it plucked out a fish's eye and swallowed it.

Uggh! she thought. I can't watch this! Forgetting her fear, she climbed to her feet and charged down the beach, yelling: "Shoo! Shoo! Go away, you horrible thing! Go away!"

With a screech of outrage the vulture abandoned its feast and took to the air. But as it flapped away across the lake, something else caught Sammie's eye. She stopped, scarcely daring to believe what she saw. She closed her eyes and opened them again and it was still there.

Nosing into view round the cliffs at the end of the cove came a small fishing boat with a dirty brown sail. It was too far away for Sammie to be able to see who was in it, but she didn't need to. It was a boat and that was enough. Yelling at the top of her lungs and madly waving her arms, she ran to the water's edge.

At first she thought that whoever was in it must be deaf, or looking the other way, for it seemed to be sailing straight on across the mouth of the cove. But she continued to wave and shout until her arms ached and her voice was hoarse, and at long last the little boat began to change course and head towards the shore.

When it was still some way off she dashed out through the shallows, tripping and stumbling and crying with relief until the water was up to her chest and she was level with the boat and gazing up into the crooked, dusky face and deep brown eyes – of Jandus.

"Oh, Jandus," Sammie cried as he heaved her on board. "Oh, Jandus!" It was all she could say as the tears of relief streamed down her face.

The little fisherman said nothing. He just smiled his lopsided smile and steered the boat in towards the shore. Then the stench hit him and he screwed up his face like a gargoyle. Sammie couldn't help giggling through her tears.

As the keel struck the bottom, there was a loud groan. Sammie looked down to see that what she'd thought was a heap of sacking was, in fact, a body. There was the glint of a jewelled dagger-handle as the body groaned again and rolled over.

"Helio!" she gasped in horror and delight. A lump came into her throat and it was all she could do not to start crying again.

"You know?" said Jandus.

Sammie nodded. "Is he all right?"

"We see," said Jandus, climbing out of the boat. With some difficulty he hoisted the still unconscious body over his shoulder and set off up the beach to the foot of the cliffs. There he laid Helio on the sand and knelt down beside him. After a brief examination he stood up and declared: "Arm broke."

"What do we do?" asked Sammie anxiously.

"We mending," said Jandus. He trotted down to the boat, scanning the ground as he went. A minute or two later he returned with a leather satchel and a

155

couple of spokes from the back of the chair.

Sammie watched as he snapped the spokes in half and tied them together in two pairs with twine from his satchel. Guessing what was coming next, she turned away. There was a grating sound and a loud groan from Helio. When she looked back again his arm was set in two splints and tightly bound with strips torn from his tunic.

"All better," said Jandus, beaming. "Leave him sleep now." He led Sammie a little way away and they sat down on the sand. He delved in the satchel and produced what looked like a dry white stick.

"Hungry?" he enquired.

"Starving," Sammie replied. "What is it?"

"Salty fish!" said Jandus smacking his lips.

Oh, no, thought Sammie. Just what I need. It looked leathery and most unappetizing. But she didn't want to offend him so she took it anyway and bit off a tiny piece. To her surprise, it was only a little salty and slightly sweet. It softened the minute it touched her tongue. She chewed and swallowed.

"Mmmm…" she said. "Not bad!"

Jandus beamed and offered her some more.

When she'd eaten her fill and drunk deeply from Jandus's water-flask, she stretched out on the sand. She was safe again, for the moment at least. Her stomach was full. And she was reunited with Helio – or would be when he woke up. But what about Mick? She realized with a sudden sharp pang of guilt that she hadn't given him a second thought since setting eyes on Jandus and Helio. Now, although it was mostly his fault he was here in the first place, she couldn't help feeling terribly responsible for him. She was surprised to find herself shivering with real dread at the thought that he might have drowned. The lump rose in her throat again.

"You didn't see anyone else, Jandus, did you?" she asked.

Jandus shook his head, so she explained about Mick.

"Other ship?" he said hesitantly when she'd finished.

"What other ship?" asked Sammie.

"Big ship – red sail."

Heart of the Valley! Of course! She'd been following behind. Maybe she'd been able to pick up survivors – and maybe, just maybe, Mick had been one of them…

"So, how did you find us?" she asked.

Jandus explained that he'd set off very early that morning to try and find a place where there might still be fish to catch. Then a little bird had landed on the boat. It had seemed very excited and after a while he'd realized that it wanted him to follow it. In due course it had led him to Helio, washed up on a stretch of rocks, and then to Sammie.

"What sort of bird was it?" asked Sammie.

"Lake bird," said Jandus. "Krrik-krrik."

So there was someone still on her side, after all! "We'll be with you!" Sammie remembered the Weaver's faint parting cry. He had meant it, it seemed.

"That was Krrik, Jandus. He's the Weaver's messenger, from Oak Holm."

"Ah," said Jandus, nodding his head. "Wise Weaver…" Then he pointed at Helio.

"Who?" he asked.

"He's called Helio." She explained who he was.

"Ahh," said Jandus again, his eyes widening. "Masterson!" He looked at Sammie very directly for a moment, then enquired: "Where Sammie and Masterson go? How Jandus helping?"

"We have to get across the lake – if Helio's all right," Sammie replied. "And then, heaven knows…"

Sometime after dusk, the moon slid over the mountains, bloated and yellow as if it too had been tainted by the Crystal Keeper's poison. It cast a pale swathe of light down the lake, on whose faintly glittering waters rode the little fishing boat. There was not a breath of wind.

Helio dozed in the stern, his arm in a sacking sling. Jandus sat at the oars, pulling with a steady rhythm. Sammie huddled in the bows, anxiously scanning the surrounding darkness for any sign of danger.

She found herself thinking back to the moment, earlier that afternoon, when she'd realized that something had happened to Uru. It was as if her veins had suddenly filled with ice. She'd put her hand to her throat. The little carving, which normally nestled warm and dry against her skin, had felt cold and clammy. And she'd known, with sudden and dreadful certainty, that the great white owl would not be waiting on the far side of the lake to help her; that she would somehow have to find her own way to the Crystal Sanctuary, the most secret place in the whole valley. For a moment she'd felt smaller, more alone, more frightened than she'd ever been in her life.

As soon as Helio woke up properly, she'd explained her fears to him and Jandus. They held council, sitting on the beach at the little cove, and eventually decided to wait until dark, then make across the lake for the place where they guessed *Heart of the Valley* would anchor to let the defenders ashore. There they might at least get news of any more survivors of the waterspout. If they were lucky, they might also find someone who knew a little more about the forest than they did.

Now, as the moon climbed and the miles passed, the lake grew narrower and the mouth of the gorge began to take shape to their left, a dark gap between the mountains. The faint sound of rushing water came through the stillness of the night.

They were close to the opposite shore, with its black ranks of trees standing silently down to the water's edge, when Sammie spotted the outline of the sailing ship, anchored in a small rocky bay. She leant forward and tapped Jandus on the shoulder. He looked round and altered course as Sammie gently shook Helio awake. Helio sat up with a grunt of pain. He grimaced and rubbed his arm as Sammie pointed out the ship. When they were a short distance off he gave a cautious halloo. It echoed faintly around the moonlit bay but no one answered.

"They must be asleep," Sammie suggested.

Helio shook his head. "Not all of them. Even when she's at anchor, there should be someone on watch, especially if there's any danger."

Now Jandus raised a finger to his lips as the little

boat glided into the looming shadow of *Heart of the Valley*. He made fast to the foot of a rope ladder, then drew his knife, placed it between his teeth and shinned up the side.

For what seemed like an eternity, Sammie and Helio sat listening to the slap of water at the hull, the gentle creaking of timbers and the occasional cry of a nightbird from the shore. Then, at last, Jandus's head appeared above them, leaning out over the side.

"Come you," he called down softly. "Empty. All empty."

Climbing a swaying rope ladder in the darkness with one arm in a sling proved almost too much for Helio. But eventually, cursing and panting, he stumbled on to the deck.

"Are you all right?" whispered Sammie.

"As long as I don't have to do that too often," he replied through clenched teeth.

In the eerie silence, *Heart of the Valley* seemed identical to her sister ship. For a moment Sammie imagined she could see the captain and his crew again, frozen in terror as the waterspout struck. She shivered and stepped closer to Helio as Jandus led them around the shadowy, deserted deck. A cloud began to cross the moon.

"Where is everyone?" she whispered nervously.

"Gone," Jandus replied without turning round. "Follow, please." He led them down a narrow stairway into the darkness of a large cabin. There he uncovered the lantern he was carrying to reveal the signs of a struggle. A table was overturned amidst a chaos of broken plates and dishes, bottles and tankards. Bedding was strewn across the floor in a scattering of feathers. Clothing lay higgledy-piggledy as if its owners had been surprised while dressing. An unpleasant smell, like rotten vegetables, lingered on the air.

Sammie and Helio stood in the flickering lantern light and looked at one another in silent dismay while Jandus briefly inspected the cabin. But it seemed there were no clues to be had, for when he had finished he simply raised his eyebrows and shrugged.

"We go," he said abruptly.

"Good idea," said Sammie. Every minute that passed made her feel more uncomfortable. She could hardly wait to get off the eerie, deserted ship. Something very nasty had happened here, she was sure of it. She turned to leave and something caught her eye. With her heart in her mouth, she bent down and lifted an upturned stool. Beneath it lay Mick's baseball cap.

She held it up without a word, a terrible sinking

feeling inside her.

Helio looked at her. Then his good arm crept around her shoulders and he said gently: "At least he didn't drown." He glanced once more round the cabin. "And it doesn't look as if anyone's been hurt here. Taken prisoner maybe, but not hurt..." He gave her a reassuring squeeze. "He might be all right, you know. Come on. Let's get out of here."

"Yes, let's," she said.

As she climbed the stairway a shaft of moonlight fell at her feet and she noticed that the steps were glistening strangely. She looked closer and saw that they were covered with sticky trails, as if huge slugs or snails had heaved themselves up the stairs.

"Wh-what d'you think made those?" she asked, pointing out the trails to Helio. He was about to answer when Jandus appeared at the top of the stairs, beckoning to them urgently.

Stepping out into the moonlight, Sammie noticed now that the whole deck was glistening with trails. They seemed to come from every corner of the ship before meeting and vanishing, all together, over the stern. But it was not the trails that concerned Jandus. He was crouching at the side and pointing towards the procession of tiny lights that had begun to spill from the dark mouth of the gorge.

On and on they came, winding their way along the shore of the lake in an ever-lengthening cavalcade. The more Sammie looked the more uneasy she grew. There was something strange about them, an unearthly green glimmer that lacked the flickering warmth of lanterns or torches.

"Marshy lights," said Jandus in an uneasy whisper. "They marshy lights. Jandus see this lights, one time ago. Now come this ship. We go."

He bent low and made for the other side of the darkened deck. Halfway across he let out an oath and leapt sideways. Sammie stifled a scream as a shadowy figure stepped out from behind the mast. Helio fumbled for his dagger and moved protectively in front of her, then a voice called out softly:

"Sammie? Is that you?"

"Mick?" Sammie's heart was hammering in her chest. "Oh, Mick! Oh, thank goodness! You gave us such a fright!" She felt suddenly faint with relief.

"It's all right," she called to Jandus who was now crouching in front of Mick, a knife glinting in one outstretched hand. "He's one of us – the one I told you about."

Jandus nodded and sheathed his knife as Mick stepped into the moonlight. Mick scowled at the little fisherman, then glanced at Sammie and Helio, a glint of satisfaction entering his eye as he noticed Helio's broken arm.

"Hello," he said, sounding not particularly pleased to see them. "I had to be quite sure you weren't the – um – whatever it was that took everybody else away."

"We thought they'd got you too!" said Sammie.

"What were they?" asked Helio.

"I don't know," said Mick. "I never saw them. I was hiding. But they made the weirdest shuffling noise – and there was an awful rotten smell…" He stopped, his eyes widening as he caught sight of the lights moving along the lakeside. "Oh, no! That's what I saw – when they came!" An edge of panic crept into his voice. "We'd better get out of here!"

Jandus nodded, looking distinctly alarmed. But Helio held up a hand.

"I think we should wait and see what they're going to do," he said. "They may not be coming out here. If so, we're as safe here as anywhere and we can just sit tight till they've gone." He looked at Mick. "You actually saw the lights – coming across the water?"

Mick nodded.

"We'll have a bit of warning, then," said Helio.

"How coming?" Jandus asked. "In boats?"

"No," said Mick. "They swam. Then slithered or

climbed up the sides. Some of them could walk."

"But I thought you said you didn't see anything," said Sammie.

Mick hesitated. "Um, no – but I – er – heard them."

"So tell us what happened," said Helio.

At first Mick seemed reluctant. He fiddled with his glasses and shuffled his feet. He must still be upset by it all, Sammie thought. When he began speaking, he stared into the darkness, avoiding anyone's eye.

After the waterspout had struck and he'd been thrown overboard, he said, he clung to a broken timber with a couple of other sailors and eventually *Heart of the Valley* arrived and they were fished out of the lake. He was given a bunk and fell asleep straightaway, exhausted by the hours in the water. When he woke up again, it was the middle of the night. The ship was anchored here by the forest, the fighting men had set off for the gorge, and the few crew who remained were all asleep.

He'd gone up on deck to get some fresh air and that was when he saw the lights coming across the water and heard things starting to slither up the side of the ship. He guessed straightaway that the defence of the gorge had failed, he said. Anyway, luckily for him he was right by a rope locker. He scrambled inside and closed the door – and there he stayed, hardly daring to breathe. He paused and glanced across the deck, then added: "Of course, I didn't have time to warn anyone."

Sammie looked at him as she handed him his cap. "I found this down in the cabin," she said. "That's why we thought they'd got you."

"Oh!" He seemed flustered. "Oh, that's where it was. I've been looking for it." He jammed it back on his head. "Anyway – they didn't get me, did they? I was lucky."

Yes, thought Sammie, you were. The only one, in fact. She was beginning to get the feeling that something in Mick's story didn't add up. She cast her mind back to the scene in the cabin, looking for clues, and found herself thinking of the spilt feathers.

"You didn't see or hear anything of Uru – the owl?" she asked. "He was supposed to be waiting for us…"

"No," said Mick.

"You're quite sure? You didn't even hear anyone talking about him?"

"I said no," Mick replied.

"Oh, well," said Sammie. "I'm glad we've found you, anyway."

Mick looked coldly at Helio. "Are you really?" he said.

With the greatest effort, Sammie held her tongue. This was not the time for a row – not when they still had to get ashore, then find the Crystal Sanctuary, and then… She glanced at the three of them. Helio, roguishly handsome with his broken arm and his fine dagger at his belt. Loyal Jandus, grubby and weather-beaten and quick with his knife. Mick with his surly expression, his specs and silly hat. They seemed such an unlikely trio that for a moment she almost laughed.

"Anyone got any ideas what we do next?" she asked.

Chapter 15

Sark the Sawback

As the last of the ghostly lights was swallowed up by the forest and darkness settled on the lake shore once more, they slipped down the side of *Heart of the Valley* and into Jandus's little boat. With scarcely a splash from the oars, Jandus rowed them across the still, black water. A short time later they were standing in the shadow of the trees while the little fisherman, waist deep in the lake, filled the boat with big stones and with tears rolling down his cheeks, watched it sink gradually out of sight.

It had been Helio who had realized, as they crouched on the deck of the ship, that the answer to their problem might be glimmering before their very eyes. If this really was the marsh army, then surely it was on its way to the Crystal Sanctuary and all they had to do was follow it – at a safe distance – through the forest. Mick turned pale and began to mutter about going back to the castle to get help, but the others quickly overruled him, and it was Jandus himself who suggested they should sink the boat so as to leave no clue for anybody – or anything – that might come along behind them.

Now, as the ripples spread away, they turned their backs on the lake and set off hurriedly after the lights which were still just visible, flitting dimly through the silent blackness of the forest ahead. Helio led the way, then came Sammie, then Mick. Jandus brought up the rear.

In time, their eyes grew used to the darkness and Sammie realized that they were following a path, winding its way through the tall, shadowy trees. At last, she thought, they were on their way to the place she dreaded most in the whole universe. She felt another flash of anger at the Master and Dame and their rotten magic that wouldn't take no for an answer. How can they expect me to do this for them? she asked herself. It's ridiculous and dangerous and they've no right… Then the anger was gone, replaced by a wretched, empty feeling of fear and helplessness that made her want to lie down on the forest floor and close her eyes and forget about the whole thing for ever.

Sunk in her own thoughts, Sammie scarcely noticed as the path began to narrow and the trees gradually closed in around them. Soon they were treading softly through a world of dark flitting shadows and strange, murky shapes. Unseen bodies rustled in the undergrowth. Small feet pattered incessantly across the forest floor. From time to time there came the sudden hoot of a bird or the shriek of some small animal. And still the lights wavered distantly through the gloom ahead of them.

It was only when the darkness began to lessen and the first hint of light started to steal through the trees, that Sammie looked up from her reverie and realized that they must have been on the march for most of the night. They came into a small clearing and halted as Helio held up his hand. He turned round and whispered in frustration: "I can't see the lights any longer. I think they've gone out. Now what do we do?"

"Go home," muttered Mick under his breath.

Sammie and Helio ignored him. For a moment they looked blankly at one another, then Jandus stepped forward. He sniffed the air and said: "Marshy smell. Jandus leading now."

"But what if they've stopped?" asked Helio. "Perhaps they only travel at night. We don't want to run into them."

"Hmmm," said Jandus. Then he nodded. "So. Waiting here, please. Jandus go see."

"All right," said Helio hesitantly. "But not too far. And Jandus – be careful."

The little fisherman gave a brief grin, then set off at a trot. Moments later he had vanished down the path.

The dawn was gathering quickly now. As the light grew stronger, mist began to rise from the ground and drift through the trees. Helio glanced around uneasily. The minutes passed and Jandus didn't reappear. Within a short while, Sammie could scarcely see across the clearing. She shivered and moved closer to Helio who was now peering anxiously into the gloom. Mick stood with his hands deep in his pockets and stared uncomfortably at the ground. They waited as the mist grew thicker and the forest sounds became more muffled, and then at last they heard a soft whistle and Jandus appeared breathlessly beside them.

"All right," he panted. "Not seeing…"

At that instant, as if from a throat full of broken bottles, came a roar:

"Staaarp! You are surrounded!"

Although they could see nothing, Sammie knew instantly that the owner of the voice was not human. At her side there was a soft hiss as Helio unsheathed his dagger. She heard Jandus's knife click open. Mick stood rooted to the spot, his face rigid with horror.

"Put down your weapons!" came the voice again,

rasping through the mist. But Jandus and Helio stood their ground and ignored the command. Sammie cowered between them, wishing she could become invisible. Mick had begun to tremble.

For a moment nothing stirred. Then there was a swirl of mist as half a dozen shapes began to glide slowly and menacingly towards them.

"So, it's fighting you want!" the voice sneered. "That's nice! We love to fight."

"Oh, yes, we do," sniggered another. "We sharpen our teeth."

"We crackle and crunch," a third snickered.

"Bones and marrow, bones and marrow," chanted a fourth, and a peal of horrid laughter rattled around the clearing.

Mick let out a strangled cry and took to his heels. Through the gloom, Sammie just had time to glimpse a flat, knobbly head with a long, broad snout, then Helio stepped forward and jabbed with his dagger. There was a loud howl followed by a tumult of snarls and grunts, and their attackers closed in.

Sammie dropped to the ground and lay there, curled up in a terrified ball, as Helio and Jandus stabbed and slashed at the writhing shapes around them. But in a little while the fighting began to move away and she looked up to find herself staring at a gap in the mist, directly ahead. Petrified as she was, she guessed this was her only chance. She rose from the ground and dashed headlong for the opening.

She was almost there when a pair of clammy, leathery arms shot round her waist from behind. She felt herself being lifted off her feet and clasped against a hard, scaly stomach.

"And what have we here?" hissed a voice in her ear as Sammie struggled in vain to break free. There was a stink of rotten vegetables and she could feel thick, blunt claws digging into her ribs.

"Put me down!" she yelled furiously, kicking as hard as she could. "Put me down, you brute!" But the thing, whatever it was, merely chuckled to itself and clasped her tighter.

Soon the sounds of fighting died away and an ominous silence fell. At the same time Sammie felt a tiny draught of air against her cheek. For a moment the mist swirled before her. Then it began to lift.

"Now we see what we caught," sneered the thing.

As daylight returned, Sammie's heart sank. Stumbling towards her, pale-faced and dishevelled, their clothes torn and bloodstained, came Helio and Jandus. Around them strode half a dozen marsh creatures whose appearance sent prickles up and down Sammie's spine. More were now appearing from the trees at the clearing's edge. Some were saw-backs, alligator-like things with pale yellow eyes bulging like carbuncles on top of their flat, warty heads. The others were huge lizards with mottled greeny-grey skin and long, slim tongues flickering in and out from their pointed snouts.

As the leading party drew near, a tall sawback gave the two captives a shove that sent them sprawling. Helio landed on his broken arm and let out a sharp cry of pain.

Sammie's captor walked forward, still clutching her to him in a vice-like grip.

"Look what I got, Sark!" he said smugly, dumping her on the ground beside her companions.

"Well, well, well," said the tall sawback. "What a surprise!" He looked at them for a moment, then moved towards Sammie and prodded her with his foot.

"You," his broken-bottle voice crackled through the silence, "what are you and why shouldn't we eat you right now?"

At the word "eat" a hubbub broke out as the swamp creatures jumped up and down, sniggering and drooling and poking one another in the ribs.

"Quiet, you bog scum!" yelled Sark.

The creatures fell silent and looked on intently as

he crouched down at Sammie's side and thrust his long, warty snout into her face. She could see a greenish spittle running between his huge, jagged teeth. His foul breath rose up her nostrils as he hissed: "Well, what are you?"

"I … I'm a girl," Sammie stammered in terror. "I'm called Sammie and I come from – the town." Heaven only knew what would happen if they found out she was a Beyonder. She held her breath as Sark stared at her, a glint of wolfish cunning in his eye.

"Hrrmm," he muttered at length, "and what might a sweet, *tender* little town girl be doing in the forest?" He made such a horrible play of the word "tender" that the other creatures giggled with glee and smacked their lips.

But before Sammie could answer, there was a commotion as another lizard appeared through the trees with a body humped over its shoulder like a sack of potatoes. It was Mick.

"Found this one running away," the lizard called to Sark.

Sark stood up. "Not dead is it?" he asked.

The lizard shook its head and sniggered. "Got a fright, that's all!" It strode into the centre of the clearing and dropped Mick at Sark's feet. Mick sat up, opened his eyes and groaned with terror to find the big sawback peering at him with a puzzled look.

"I've – seen – you – somewhere – before – haven't I?" said Sark slowly.

Mick trembled and said nothing as Sark scratched his rump with one horny claw. Then he threw back his head and let out a guffaw that rattled away through the forest. "Oh, he's a crafty one, this one."

Sammie held her breath, not daring to say a word.

"Lost your tongue, town girl?" asked Sark with a nasty grin. "Don't you want to know what he did?"

Sammie avoided his eye and said nothing.

"Well, I'll tell you, anyway." Sark gave another guffaw. "It was the owl, of course! He told us about the owl – didn't you, crafty boy?" He bent down and poked Mick with his claw. Mick shrank away.

"He was on the ship, he was," Sark went on, obviously enjoying himself. "The first one we caught. Wandering about on deck, weren't you?" He winked at Mick. "Well! He thought we were going to scrunch him. Got so frightened he said he'd tell us something really helpful if we promised to let him be. And so he did. Ho, yes! Told us the owl was down in the cabin, talking to the captain. So we put a net over the doorway – and caught us a nice big white surprise!"

"Oh, no!" Sammie could no longer contain her dismay. The feathers in the cabin! She could picture it all now – the chaos as the crew were quickly over-powered, and the creatures pointing and leering as Uru – poor Uru – struggled to break free of the net.

Mick hung his head and looked as if he wanted the earth to swallow him. Jandus glared at him and drew his finger across his throat. Helio simply shook his head slowly and wearily.

"He was right, of course," Sark went on. "We *were* going to scrunch him an' all – but he slipped away and hid somewhere when we were all in a tangle with the owl. So we let him be…" He paused, smacking his lips. "But now we've found him again, we might just scrunch him anyhow –" he jabbed a claw at Sammie, Helio and Jandus – "and you with him."

"Oh, yes, yes!" clamoured the rabble. "Scrunch 'em all! Bones and marrow! Bones and marrow!"

Mick had begun to tremble uncontrollably.

"But then again," continued the big sawback, shaking his head in mock sympathy, "seeing as how my master wants you so bad – p'raps we'd better not!"

There was a groan of disappointment from the creatures. A cruel grin flickered down Sark's long jaw.

"Ho yes, my beauties, old Sark knows just who you are! Knew it as soon as I saw the Beyonder here, didn't I! *Tender* little thing…" He let out another cackle of laughter.

"But Sarky!" called one of the lizards. "How would our master ever know if we scrunched 'em?"

"'E never would," said another.

"No, he'd never," hissed a third. "And we're starvin', we are…" It stepped a little closer.

"Stay where you are, marsh-slime!" roared Sark.

"But Sarky," persisted the lizard, "we ain't 'ad a square meal in days."

"Not for days and days," said the second.

"I say scrunch 'em now!" called a sawback, taking a shuffling pace forward.

"Yes, now!" called another, following suit.

"Didn't I say, stay where you are?" shouted Sark. But his voice was less commanding this time, and a thoughtful look had entered his eye.

The second sawback, in any case, paid no attention. "If 'e asks, just say we never found 'em." It shuffled forward another couple of paces.

"Yes, 'cos he'd never know," called the first lizard, and a couple of others took up the refrain:

"He'd-never-know, he'd-never-never-know!"

There was a flickering of tongues and a smacking of chops as the rest of the creatures began to move into the centre of the clearing.

Sark glanced at the four captives, then at the advancing creatures, then back to the captives again. His yellow eyes narrowed. He licked his lips. "Hrrmm…"

It was all the greedy reptiles needed. They lurched forwards in a babbling, grunting rabble and before Sark could even open his mouth, they'd knocked him flat and were trampling over him in their eagerness to get at Sammie and the others.

Mick gave a shriek of terror as the first claw reached for his ankle. Sammie shrank away and closed her eyes. Then the clearing rang to a sudden cry of "STOP!"

Muttering and cursing and bumping into one another, the rabble halted in astonishment as before them, Helio heaved himself to his feet, his good hand upraised as if daring them to take another step. With his pale face, his tattered clothes, and his broken arm in its dirty sling, he looked more dead than alive, but his voice was steady as he held the reptiles' gaze and said slowly:

"Your … master … knows … everything. Everything! If you so much as touch us he'll know about it." He took a pace towards the creatures. They edged back, peering at him uncertainly. "In fact, he probably knows you've found us already. Eat us now and that'll be the end of you. He'll simply destroy you." He snapped his fingers. "Just like that." A couple of reptiles jumped nervously. "Take my word for it…" He swayed, then sat down heavily on the ground.

Whether the rest of the creatures believed Helio or not, it seemed that Sark at least did. By this time he was back on his feet again and eager to restore authority. He elbowed his way, cursing and scowling, to the front of the rabble. There he nodded sourly to Helio, then turned to his cowardly followers and bellowed: "Can't trust you for a second, can I? One more moment and you'd all've been swamp pie. 'Course our master knows everything. Ho yes! And if you'd given me half a chance, I'd have told you meself. So now it's quick march to the Crystal Sanctuary. Let *him* decide what to do with 'em when we get there."

"Maybe he'll give us a reward," hissed one of the lizards hopefully.

"Couple o' prisoners from that World's Edge would do nicely," muttered another.

"Enough of that talk!" roared Sark. "It'll get us all disappeared."

"It will indeed," said Helio, climbing unsteadily to his feet again. He stared at Sark and said quietly:

"Just as a precaution, don't you think it would be a good idea to let me have my dagger back?"

Sark scratched his head and muttered to himself, then he rounded on the creatures and barked: "Find him his weapon, someone! Double quick! Then we'll be off. Jump to it, you sons-of-leeches!"

A few minutes later, with the big sawback at its head, the procession of swamp creatures and humans left the clearing and the forest closed in around them again. Sammie and Helio walked side by side. Then came Jandus. A few paces behind him trudged Mick, his head bowed.

"Are you all right?" whispered Sammie to Helio.

"More or less." He rubbed his arm and grimaced. "What about you?"

"I – I think so," Sammie replied. She was still shaking, she realized. "I really thought we'd had it back there, you know. But you were…"

Helio shook his head and smiled palely. "I couldn't let them eat you yet – not while you've still got a job to do!"

Sammie tried unsuccessfully to return the smile. "No," she said, "I s'pose not."

Chapter 16

The Crystal Sanctuary

All day they walked through the gloom of the deep forest, seeing nothing and hearing nothing. From time to time Sammie, Helio and Jandus exchanged a few whispered words, and at midday they shared some dried fish. But Mick refused food and said nothing. Around them, the reptiles padded softly along on their horny feet.

Dusk was settling when Sark quickened his pace. A few minutes later, a pale green glow began to spill through the trees and the faint clamour of voices drifted towards them.

"I think we've arrived," whispered Helio.

As the glow grew brighter and the clamour louder, Sammie felt as if she was shrinking inside.

"I'm frightened, Helio," she whispered.

Helio said nothing but reached for her hand and squeezed it. At that moment, from somewhere above her head, she heard a particular sound:

"Krrik-krrik." The cry came once only.

She glanced up and for a second caught a shimmer of white wings, high in the branches of a nearby tree. Then they were gone. She looked around but nobody else seemed to have noticed the little bird.

"I've just seen Krrik!" she whispered to Helio.

"Are you sure?"

She nodded several times and he gave a quick smile. "So the Weaver must know where we are!" He turned to Jandus and passed on the news.

The trees were thinning now and the path had widened into a track that seemed to head down into the green glow. But instead of following the track, as Sammie had expected, they now turned on to a smaller trail that led off to one side. The reason soon became clear as out of the darkness loomed a tumble of enormous moss-covered boulders, framing the dark opening of an archway.

Sammie's blood ran cold as she noticed the two huge shapes that sat stock still, one on either side of the opening, and she found herself grimly recalling Helio's words: "…there wasn't a wolf to be seen in the valley – and there's never been one since!" For the motionless guardians of the archway were two immense, black wolves. Their eyes smouldered like live coals in the gloom, and they bared their fangs and growled deep in their throats as the reptiles and their captives drew near. Then Sark stepped forward and spoke. The wolves nodded and Sark beckoned to the others to follow.

They passed through the archway and emerged close to the edge of a low cliff. Below was a shallow valley teeming with creatures and people, all bathed in a cold, green flickering light. As Sammie gazed down at this unearthly scene, wondering what terrible power the Crystal Keeper wielded, the light suddenly dimmed and a shriek of laughter crackled out of the gloom. She froze.

For what seemed like an age the laughter rang amongst the rocks around them. But at last it died away and in its place came the voice of a man. It was a voice that had once been strong and clear, but now there was madness in it.

"And who have we here?" it inquired softly.

The big sawback snapped to attention. "Sark the Sawback, Master. And your … er … visitors."

"Oh, yes," came the voice, as if it had forgotten. "My visitors. My most determined visitors. Well, well, well…"

The voice paused, then continued more briskly: "Thank you, Sark. You may go now."

Sark hesitated for a moment, a hopeful glint in his eye.

The voice rose a tone. "I said you may go."

If Sark had been expecting a reward for his efforts, he quickly thought better of it.

"Yes, Master, of course, Master," he said hastily. He turned and barked an order, then hurried away through the archway with the rest of the rabble muttering mutinously at his heels.

"Sawbacks!" exclaimed the voice contemptuously, as the last one vanished between the boulders. "And lizards! Uggh!"

Now Sammie and her companions stood alone, straining their eyes into the darkness. It seemed that they were on an enormous rocky ledge, almost as big as a stage. Somewhere, there was a noise of tinkling water. Ahead, the cliff towered up into the night. Behind, it dropped into the valley. There was only one way out and that lay through the archway and past the two watchwolves.

"So," came the voice again, "welcome to the Crystal Sanctuary. Sammie, the brave Beyonder. Noble Helio Masterson. Jandus, the humble fisherman. And Mick, the – er – fearless owl-catcher…"

The words disintegrated into another terrible cackle of laughter. Something moved in the darkness and at once they were bathed in blinding green light. Sammie thought her head was going to split in two. She clamped her eyes shut and put her hands over her face.

"Rather bright is it?" crowed the voice. "Oh, dear, how thoughtless of me."

The blaze faded. Sammie opened her eyes and found her gaze drawn to the back of the Sanctuary and the water, cascading gently from its hidden source, high up in the cliff, and tumbling away down the rock in a hundred little channels that fanned out like the wrinkles in a great carved face. Over the centuries, each one had been worn smooth and glistening as the water pursued its endless, tinkling course out of the darkness and down into the glimmering pool that swept round the foot of the cliff at the rear of the Sanctuary in the slim crescent shape of a perfect new moon.

It would have been the most beautiful place Sammie had ever seen, were it not for the bitter green light that streamed from the depths of the pool, chilling her to the bone and making her feel as if she was shrivelling inside.

"The crystal!" she muttered to herself.

Then something else caught her eye. Like a gnarled claw, a stunted pine tree pushed its way up from between two of the great boulders at the entrance. Halfway up its withered trunk was a single branch from which hung a makeshift cage. Motion-less in the cage was the shrunken frame of what had once been a great white owl.

"Uru!" cried Sammie in horror.

"Oh, no!" choked Helio.

Mick stared at his feet, unable even to look.

"Yes," said the Crystal Keeper, walking slowly towards them. "That pestilential owl. Little did I know what trouble he would cause me."

For a moment the owl lifted its beak and one eyelid flickered. Sammie felt the tiniest flush of warmth from the little carving at her throat. Then the proud white head slumped forward again and the spark went out. She could bear the sight no longer. Trembling, she turned her gaze to the Crystal Keeper who now stood directly before them.

Tall and skeleton-thin, he was wrapped from neck to toe in dusty rags. A mane of filthy hair straggled to his shoulders. From his jaw sprouted a beard which fell almost to his chest, matted and tangled like rotting rope. But it was the eyes that made Sammie's blood run cold. Maddened and bloodshot, they glared at her from deep in their sockets as the Crystal Keeper spoke again:

"You have been lucky, Beyonder. Luckier than you deserve. But that luck has deserted you now, as it did your friend there..." he pointed a long finger at the cage, "...and as it must at last desert all who pit themselves against the power of the crystal."

He paused for a moment with the sickly green light flickering across his gaunt face. Sammie shuddered to see a faint twitching of the rags at his chest, as if they concealed some living thing. Then he went on:

"Of course I knew of you the moment you arrived. The hare – yes, the harmless, lolloping hare – he told me. I was not much concerned for I knew even then that my power was great. But I sent the bats for good measure, and the owl interfered, meddlesome bird. Then, when I learnt from the raven where you were making for, I alerted the bear – a poor choice, I admit, for they are stupid creatures. After that I merely waited until I knew I had your attention and then – I blew you back to Beyond – just like this..."

The Crystal Keeper suddenly turned his gaze on Mick. Sammie watched Mick's head lift as if drawn irresistibly upwards by a magnet. The madman's mouth was thin and hard as a whetstone and his eyes stared wider and wider. For a moment Mick stood in trembling silence. Then, with a cry of pure terror, he vanished into thin air.

The Crystal Keeper chuckled cruelly as Sammie and Helio looked at one another in horror. "But then," he went on, "they called you back – and who should come with you this time but your bungling fool of a brother." He snapped his fingers and Mick instantly reappeared, looking dazed and terrified out of his wits.

"So I sent the waterspout," continued the Crystal Keeper, "and *again* you survived. Now I grew curious and I asked myself: what could it be that would make four miserable ants set themselves against the might of the Crystal Keeper? But I could find no answer."

He paused again and fixed Sammie with an icy stare.

"Now that you are here, *you* will give me the answer. What was it, Sammie the Beyonder? What was it that brought you here?"

Sammie racked her brains but could think of nothing. Eventually, in despair, she blurted out the only thing she could think of – the truth.

"I came to cure you," she said, feeling small and foolish and more frightened than she'd ever been in her life.

At this the Crystal Keeper threw back his head and laughed till the tears rolled down his hollow cheeks and into his beard.

"You – came – to – *cure* – me?" he guffawed, clutching his shaking sides. "But you, little worm, are not a physician and I, the Crystal Keeper, am not ill. Oh, no! I am full of power!"

"Then why don't you use it for the good of our valley, the way the crystal ought to be used," exploded Helio, suddenly finding his voice. He reached for his dagger, but before he could draw it there was a thunderous crack, a bolt of light flew from the Crystal Keeper's outstretched fingers, and Helio was flung across the Sanctuary. He hit the ground with a yelp of pain and there lay pinned and writhing under a shimmering green shroud.

"Speak when you're spoken to, maggot!" roared the Crystal Keeper. He turned around and strode to a great tree stump, crudely carved to the shape of a throne. He flung himself into it and drummed his fingers furiously on his knees. His eyes darted hither and thither. There was another little quivering amongst the rags at his chest, as if something was crawling about inside them.

Trapped by the light, Helio wriggled and flapped on the ground like a wounded insect. Then there was a soft hiss, the light vanished, and he sat up with a dazed look. Gingerly, Jandus helped him to his feet, keeping one fearful eye on the Crystal Keeper all the while.

In the silence that followed, Sammie gathered all her courage and hesitantly addressed the figure on the throne.

"Surely you don't want to destroy the valley? It's a happy, beautiful place. The Master and Dame are good people. And you were once…" she corrected herself hastily "…you are the Crystal Keeper. Can't you remember how it was before … er … before…"

Not knowing how to continue, she gestured vaguely at the Sanctuary, the valley beyond, the Crystal Keeper himself, and for a moment a curious look clouded his face, as if some deep and long-forgotten memory was stirring. Then, like a feather in the wind, it was gone. He shook his head and his eyes flashed as he demanded:

"What need have I of happiness and beauty? They are nothing to me. I will consume them – as I consume everything with my great and terrible power. I will strip the valley of all that has gone before, and then I will shape it again in my image, so that I am the valley and the valley is I." His voice was rising and growing louder. "You have no power, little Beyonder! The Master and Dame are nothing but fools – a fumbling greybeard and a chattering busybody!"

Helio bristled but Jandus gripped his arm. The Crystal Keeper continued: "It is I who control the crystal, not they. Tomorrow they will learn of real power when they hang from their gibbets and see their fine castle in flames. Yes, tomorrow at sunset, when my army marches out from the forest and the town falls to the Crystal Keeper, the mightiest ruler this valley has ever known…"

His words rang through the Sanctuary as he rocked back and forth in his throne, his eyes blazing. Then, all at once, an agonized look came over his face. He clasped his hands to his head and let out a long, low groan. He slumped back against the throne with his eyes closed and twisted his head this way and that as if to shake off some terrible pain.

Eventually he heaved himself from his seat and stumbled across to the pool. There he scooped up water in cupped hands and drank feverishly. Then he scooped again and tipped water over his head, rubbing it into his skull as it trickled through his filthy, tangled locks. At last he staggered back to his throne again and sat down.

In the silence that followed there came a sudden soft squeaking and a further movement amongst the Crystal Keeper's rags. A moment later a tiny brown mouse appeared at his shoulder. It scampered down his arm and perched on his knee, gazing up at him with nose and whiskers twitching expectantly. Sammie hardly dared look, guessing that at any moment he would dash it to the rocky floor, or lift it up and crush it in his hand. But instead, to her amazement, he sank further back into the throne and with half closed eyes fumbled inside his rags to produce some titbit which he offered to the little creature. At once it began to nibble from his fingertips, and as it did so he stroked its head and muttered softly: "Mousey, my friend. Oh, Mousey, Mousey."

For several minutes he appeared to be oblivious of anyone but himself and his tiny companion. Then the mouse scurried back up his sleeve and vanished inside his rags again. A moment later he flung himself forward in the throne and gazed at his captives, eyes wide and staring.

"This audience is at an end," he said coldly. "I will decide upon the manner of your destruction in the morning."

He turned towards the boulders and called out: "Fang! Claw! Be present!"

At once the two huge wolves came bounding through the archway. They stopped by the throne, their smouldering eyes fixed on their master.

"Take our prisoners to World's Edge and guard

them well. I wish them back here at dawn. Now go!"

The wolves nodded in unison. Then, with menacing growls, they herded Sammie, Helio, Mick and Jandus across the rocky stage to where the shadowed mouth of a passage opened in the cliff-face. There, Fang moved ahead and Claw fell behind as the four prisoners stepped out of the baleful green light of the Crystal Sanctuary and into the darkness.

Chapter 17

World's Edge

For a short while they seemed to be heading straight into the centre of the cliff. They could hear water running close by and Sammie imagined it must be the stream that fed the crystal pool. But then the sound grew fainter and at the same time the passage began to lead them upwards.

Every so often they came across a torch, guttering and smoking in the stale air. Sammie was glad of the light. It made the panicky, breathless feeling of being underground a little easier to bear. But then she noticed the huge spiders' webs overhead, quivering gently as their owners sat in wait, and she longed to be back in the darkness again.

In due course the way became steeper and the rough, rocky floor gave way to steps. The sound of the stream had gone now and they could hear only their own footsteps and the soft padding of paws, as the great black shadows led them up through the gloom, fangs bared and red eyes burning.

On and on they climbed until it seemed to Sammie that they must have left the forest far below, and that now they must surely be somewhere high in the very heart of the mountains. Her legs were beginning to ache and the breath was rasping in her throat when she sensed at last that the path was levelling out again. The air began to freshen and shortly they found themselves in a long, well-lit tunnel.

At the far end of the tunnel, a great wooden door was set into the rock. On a stool by the door sat a man, one of the Crystal Keeper's slaves, Sammie guessed. His clothes were tattered and dirty, but from a thick leather belt around his waist hung a single, enormous key, glinting in the torchlight. He seemed to be asleep, but as they drew near he opened one eye, rose slowly from his stool and unlocked the door. It swung open to reveal what looked like a small, dark cave.

"Welcome to World's Edge," he muttered gruffly, gesturing into the shadows.

For a moment they hesitated on the threshold. Then there was a growl at their backs and Helio stepped forward. As Sammie followed him she glanced behind to see the wolves settling down on their haunches, one on either side of the doorway, like great ebony statues in the wavering torchlight.

The heavy door swung to with an echoing thud. The key rattled in the lock.

Then there was silence.

As they stood together in the darkness, Sammie could feel a great weight of despair in her heart. It was as if the huge mass of the mountain was settling down around them, to bury them here for ever. They would never escape this place – and even if by some miracle they did, what would they do then? The minute she had set eyes on the Crystal Keeper she'd known her mission was impossible, that it had all been in vain from the start. So tomorrow – or maybe it was today now – he would destroy them, and she would never see Mere Cottages or her mother again. She felt a sob rising, but it got lost in her throat. She was beyond tears.

Helio took her hand and drew her away from the door. Her legs felt like lead, but she allowed him to guide her on. They left the cave and entered a low passage which gave a twist, then a turn, and suddenly there was a glimmer of light ahead. A few moments later they were stepping out into an immense cavern, as big as a cathedral. Its gaping mouth framed a clear night sky, shimmering with galaxies of stars.

A huddle of sleeping bodies lay on the rocky floor before them. But the companions scarcely noticed as they walked towards the mouth of the cavern – and froze. For there, beneath the twinkling heavens, the floor met thin air and plummeted endlessly into a dark abyss that seemed to cleave the mountains to their very core.

"World's Edge," muttered Helio.

Sammie nodded hopelessly. She stood on the brink, gazing down into the yawning blackness. For a moment she was tempted by the idea of the one little step that would end it all there and then. But even in the depths of her despair there was something that chided her for such a thought and she found her mind turning instead to Uru in his cage, way down in the forest below them. An instant later she felt the faintest tingling at the base of her throat. It was as if a tiny tremor was running through the little fishbone carving.

She took several paces back from the edge. "We've *got* to do something!" she burst out.

As her words rang round the cavern some of the sleeping prisoners rolled over and sat up, muttering and rubbing their eyes.

"But what?" asked Helio, gesturing vaguely at the acres of cold, dark rock. His eyes were glazed with fatigue and pain.

"I don't know yet," Sammie replied. "There must be something! Think!"

Now several of the prisoners clambered to their feet and began to stare curiously. Jandus still stood by the abyss, lost in thought. Mick, meanwhile, had wandered off to the other side of the cavern and slumped down against the wall as if he no longer cared what happened.

Sammie closed her eyes and racked her brains for a way out, but none came. The despair was beginning to return when she felt a tugging at her sleeve. It was Jandus. There was an intense expression on his nutbrown face as he pointed back towards the passage cave and whispered: "You make key-man open door and…" he drew his hand across his throat "…Jandus take care of wolfs."

"But how, Jandus?" she asked. "What on earth are you going to do?"

Jandus just shook his head and let slip a tiny grin. "Sammie and Masterson get key-man. Leave wolfs to me." He rooted in his satchel and produced a ball of twine, then walked back to the mouth of the cavern.

"What d'you reckon he's up to?" Sammie asked Helio.

Helio shook himself, as if to clear his head, then shrugged. "I don't know. But it'd better work, what-ever it is."

"So how are we going to get the door open…"

At that moment there was a murmur amongst the prisoners and a girl stepped forward, so frail and thin that she seemed no more than a bundle of rags. Her face was pinched with hunger and she looked as if a breath of mountain wind could knock her down. But her huge grey eyes smouldered with a strange recognition as she stared at Sammie, and said in a softly lilting voice: "You're not one of us, are you?"

"Wh-what d'you mean?" asked Sammie nervously.

"You're not from the valley."

Sammie didn't know what to reply. For a moment, the silent cavern seemed more immense than ever. Then Helio said hesitantly: "How d'you know?"

"Oh, I can tell." The girl gave a slight smile. "Some of us forest-folk … well … we … know things…"

"Hmmm. So who are you?" asked Helio.

She shrugged. "One of his prisoners, like you. Name of Marga. But that's no matter…" She gave Sammie another long, curious look, then she nodded to herself.

"You're from that Beyond or whatsit … that's what matters!" The lilt was becoming a sing-song.

"You're here to save us, you are!"

She stood staring at Sammie, her eyes enormous and vibrant in the moonlight.

Sammie's heart leapt. If this strange forest girl knew who she was and why she was here, maybe she could also tell her what to do...

"Yes I am," Sammie replied. "But Marga, I don't know how. Do you?"

The girl did not reply. Instead, she turned to face the cave-mouth and looked out into the night sky. The other prisoners, thirty or forty of them, were all on their feet now. They shuffled into a half-circle around her and watched attentively as she concentrated her gaze on the stars and a faraway look came over her.

For several minutes she stared silently into the heavens, then she turned towards Sammie and Helio again, a puzzled look on her face. She gave a long sigh and said: "Makes no sense ... no sense at all..."

"Tell us anyway," said Helio.

"Well..." she began, "what I saw were this great wind ... in the forest it was ... trees waving an' all. And then this big branch were breaking and falling down and down..." She paused for a moment. "Then there was just a man's head, all shaggy like a beast. And there were this big lump on it, under the hair you see. And the lump were full of badness, terrible badness, inside his head, like. Then the badness went an' everything were lovely … just lovely…"

Her voice had become dreamy. For a while she seemed to be staring right through Sammie without seeing her. Then she shook her head. Her eyes focused again and she repeated sadly: "Told you it made no sense, I did. I'm sorry."

But a glint had returned to Helio's eye. "I think," he said, "that it does make sense." He paused, nodding to himself. "Yes, by the Lights!" He turned to Sammie and grasped her shoulder excitedly.

"Don't you see? It's *him* – the Crystal Keeper. There must have been a storm in the forest and he got hit by a falling branch – hit on the head. That's what the lump's from … we saw how much it hurts him – back there at the Crystal Sanctuary – didn't we? So the badness that Marga saw – that must be partly the pain in his head … but I think it's also his madness, because the bang on the head didn't just hurt him, it drove him crazy, too. In fact, it's all the same thing – cure one and you cure the other!"

Sammie nodded slowly. Helio was right. She felt it in her bones.

So at last, at long last, she knew what had to be

done. But did knowing make it any better? Somehow she had to get the Crystal Keeper to place himself in her hands – and then what? She had no medicine nor any knowledge of it. She didn't even have any – what was it her mother used for bumps and bangs – witch-hazel...

"You'll be all right, you will." She found herself looking again into Marga's great grey eyes. They were smiling at her now, full of confidence and encouragement.

"Yes you will!" Helio put his good arm round Sammie and gave her a big squeeze, then turned to the gathering of prisoners and said: "We've got to get the jailer to open the door somehow. Has anyone got any ideas?"

From where Helio and Jandus stood, just inside the great wooden door, it sounded as if a riot had broken out and all the prisoners were killing each other. The din echoed up from the cavern – a tumult of furious shouts and screams and curses, ringing off the rocky walls around them. They waited a little, then Jandus began to hammer on the door.

Eventually a shutter slid back and the jailer's sleepy face appeared on the other side of the grill. Before he could say a word, Jandus started to babble urgently: "Quick, quick! Fighting! Big fighting! They killing Masterson, them prisoners. You come!"

The jailer tilted his head to listen to the racket. "Sounds like fightin' all right." His eyes narrowed. "Who you say they killin'?"

"Masterson! Mas-ter-son!" Jandus sounded beside himself. "He number one 'portant prisoner. You stop fight! Come quick!"

The shrieks and roars from the cavern were growing louder.

"Hmmm…" The jailer turned away. Through the noise, Helio thought he heard the man speaking to the two watchwolves. He held his breath in the darkness. Then came a rattle in the lock. Helio nodded to Jandus and raised his dagger.

With a creak, the door swung open, torchlight spilled into the cave and the jailer stepped hesitantly over the threshold. With all the strength in his good arm, Helio brought down the jewelled handle of his dagger on the back of the man's head. The jailer pitched forward without a sound. A moment later, a thunderous growl shook the air and Fang and Claw sprang forward, teeth bared and eyes flaming with rage.

Helio leapt back behind the door and flattened himself against the wall as Jandus stepped out from the shadows, then turned and headed like a hare for the cavern.

Moments later, with Fang and Claw in furious pursuit, he burst into the great rocky chamber. The din of the riot stopped abruptly and in the silence that followed, the prisoners stood aside to let them through. Sammie watched, her heart in her mouth, as Jandus sprinted for the edge of the cavern without so much as a backwards glance. Then, just as Fang's slavering jaws closed on his heels, the little fisherman gave a blood-curdling yell and launched himself over the precipice.

Unable to stop himself, Fang also hurtled out into the void with a gargling howl. The sound lingered hideously until the black depths of the abyss claimed him, far, far below.

But Claw had not followed his brother. He shuddered to a halt at the very brink. There he turned and crouched to face the centre of the chamber, growling horribly, his fangs bared.

At that moment Helio came panting into the cavern. The watchwolf gave a roar of rage and sprang at him. Helio held out his weapon as the colossal shape sped through the air and landed on top of him, snarling and spitting, and for a moment they rolled together on the ground in a blur of black fur. Then a swarm of prisoners fell on the great wolf, beating at him with stones and bare fists, stabbing with little knives.

But Claw's strength was immense. He rose up, arched his back and shook himself, throwing off his attackers like so many fleas. Now Sammie could see that Helio lay beneath him – dead or alive, she could not tell – with his dagger deep in Claw's haunch. But Claw seemed scarcely to notice. His great head twisted from side to side as he scanned the cavern. Then, with another fearful snarl, he launched himself across the rocky floor towards Sammie, a fury of teeth and claws and burning red eyes, the dagger still lodged in his flesh.

Sammie dropped to the ground in terror and at once the nearest prisoners threw themselves on to her, covering her with their bodies. There was a terrible impact as Claw landed on top of them. Then he was snarling and spitting and scrabbling for a way through to his prize. Within moments the rest of the prisoners were on him. They yelled and flailed and stabbed, but the great watchwolf fought on oblivious.

Half suffocated beneath the pile of protecting bodies, Sammie didn't see Helio stagger to his feet again and stumble towards the mêlée. There he stopped for a moment to steady himself, then drew a deep breath, reached out a trembling hand for the hilt of his weapon and wrenched it from the writhing black body. The watchwolf gave a howl of pain, but his furious assault scarcely faltered and still he clawed and bit and tore in his frenzy to reach Sammie.

With his dagger dangling from his hand, Helio took a couple of faltering paces back and began to circle drunkenly around the great beast. But just as he spotted his opening and began to raise his weapon again, Claw caught sight of him. The watchwolf gave a roar of rage and lashed out with one huge black paw. The blow knocked Helio to his knees and sent the dagger spinning from his hand. It clattered across the rocky floor of the cavern towards the solitary figure of Mick who still sat slumped against the far wall, watching the fighting without expression. He blinked as the dagger came to rest right before him, gazed at it for a moment, then slowly reached out for it...

"Don't!" yelled Helio, struggling in vain to get to his feet. "Leave it!"

But it was too late, for now Mick had picked it up and was turning it over in his hands. The glitter of the jewelled handle caught Claw's eye. With a furious snarl, the watchwolf turned and sprang from the writing mound of prisoners. Mick made no attempt to get out of the way. He sat with a startled look as the great black shape flew across the cavern towards him. Only at the last moment, as if he'd suddenly remembered he ought to do something, did he raise the dagger and hold it out vaguely in front of him. Then Claw thundered down on top of him and Mick disappeared from view. For a split second the huge beast seemed frozen where he had landed, his eyes smouldering and teeth bared in rage. Then, as if in slow motion, his legs began to buckle, he threw back his head with a long, terrible howl, and at last he rolled over. The dagger was sunk to the hilt in his breast.

For a moment there was silence. Then a triumphant cheer rose through the great rocky chamber and rang out over the abyss. Sammie climbed to her feet and looked across the cavern to see the prisoners dragging Mick out from under the monstrous black corpse, hoisting him on to their shoulders, shouting and singing as they reached up to shake his hand and pat him on the back, showering him with praise. At first Mick looked dazed and bewildered. He took off his spectacles and rubbed his eyes as if he'd just woken up from a long, deep sleep. But little by little a grin of pure delight began to spread across his face, until suddenly he yanked his cap off his head and, with a great whoop of glee, hurled it up towards the shadowy heights of the cavern. And as the prisoners scrambled to catch it and Mick rode aloft on their shoulders, beaming, Sammie realized that this was the first time she had ever seen him looking really, truly happy.

Then someone cried out, pointing at something, and a hush fell as they turned towards the starlit mouth of the cave. Over the edge of the cliff a hand appeared. Then an arm, and another arm. Then a familiar nutbrown face. Sammie felt weak with relief as Jandus hauled himself slowly back up the twine that was tied around his waist, and clambered out into the cave. He stood up and gave a shaky grin as the cheering began again.

Chapter 18

The Healing

Once the last prisoner was out of the cave, Mick and Jandus dragged the unconscious jailer through the doorway into the torchlit tunnel and set about tying him up. Helio limped out after them, looking pale and shaken. But his face was set as he turned and closed the great wooden door behind them. He locked it and pocketed the key.

"That's the end of World's Edge," he declared, to loud applause. "No one will ever be shut up there again."

Taking the torches from the wall to light their way, they set off for the Crystal Sanctuary and soon they were plunging down and down again through the dark heart of the mountain. With the prisoners for company, the journey passed quickly and it seemed to Sammie no time at all before they began to hear the crystal stream trickling faintly through the darkness. The knot tightened in her stomach.

A few moments later they halted at a fork in the passage. Sammie didn't remember seeing it on the way up, but it had been pitch dark then, and anyway, she'd been too lost in her own misery to notice anything else. Now Helio asked if anyone knew where the second passage went. No one did, but one of the prisoners immediately volunteered to find out. He hurried away and after an anxious few minutes reappeared to report breathlessly that it emerged in the forest, a little way back from the arch that led to Crystal Sanctuary. Helio conferred softly with Jandus for a moment. Then he turned to the prisoners and asked if they would be willing to take that route to the Sanctuary and get rid of whatever had replaced the watchwolves at the entrance, then take up guard themselves. As the prisoners nodded and muttered their agreement, Mick stepped forward and whispered to Helio.

Helio listened and a shadow of uncertainty crossed his face. He stared ahead as if trying to make up his mind about something. Then someone caught his eye from the crowd. Sammie followed his gaze and saw that Marga was looking directly at him. She gave the faintest nod. Helio broke into a decisive smile.

"Mick has offered to go with you," he said to the prisoners. "He knows the Sanctuary – he's been there before. And after his – er – heroic performance at World's Edge, I'm sure you'll be glad of his company!"

The prisoners' chorus of agreement echoed in the torchlit passage. They were smiling and nodding to each other, and some reached out to shake Mick's hand for a second time. Sammie watched the grin slide across his face again.

"You will be careful, won't you?" she said.

" 'Course I will," Mick replied with a wink. He jammed his cap firmly on his head, then set off jauntily into the darkness of the second passage. The rag-tag army of prisoners followed him, leaving Sammie, Helio and Jandus to follow the other path to the Crystal Sanctuary.

The three companions hurried down the main passage in silence. A few minutes later they stopped in the shadows on the threshold of the Sanctuary. Before them, the green glimmer was lit every so often with a brighter flicker, followed by the dull rumble of thunder. Helio moved cautiously forward and peeped around the corner.

"It's all right!" he whispered. "He's alone – and asleep. Now, Jandus and I are going to wait by the boulders in case anything tries to come through the archway before the others get here. Sammie, you wait till we're in position."

Sammie could feel her heart beginning to pound against her ribs. Her mouth was quite dry and her palms felt clammy.

"Are you ready?" Helio asked her softly.

Sammie nodded and he stepped forward to clasp both her hands in his good one. For a moment he gazed at her with his deep blue eyes, unable to find the words he wanted. A lump rose in Sammie's throat. She turned her head away and whispered: "Go on! Go on!"

Helio and Jandus slipped out of the passage and began to steal across the Sanctuary. When they were nearly at the entrance they parted and crept into place by the great boulders, Jandus on the left and Helio on the right.

Sammie waited a moment to be sure that whatever lurked on the other side of the boulders had not seen or heard them. Then she too stepped out into the pale green light of the Crystal Sanctuary.

She had gone only a few paces when a flash of lightning lit the rocky stage. She spotted the Crystal Keeper at once. He was stretched out beside the pool.

An instant later there was a loud crash of thunder. The Crystal Keeper sat bolt upright and gazed around with wildly staring eyes. Sammie froze in terror, but he seemed not to notice her. After a moment he clasped his hands to his head and sank back on the ground with a groan. Something made Sammie glance across the Sanctuary to where Uru hung in his cage. In the dismal green light she could see that his eyes were open and his beak was held forward. Although the effort was almost too much for him, he was trying to speak to her.

What was it? Something about her hands ... there was a funny, pins-and-needles feeling in them ... and a curious urge to touch the head of the figure by the pool...

She felt very confused. What did it all mean? She racked her brains and then, all at once, the memories flooded in. The special gift that the Dame had mentioned. Her grandmother's healing hands. Marga's vision of the badness inside the Crystal Keeper's head. As if the pieces of a puzzle had suddenly locked together, it all became clear. *She* had the power to heal too!

"Thank you, Uru! Thank you!" she muttered as the owl's head fell forward again on to his breast.

The storm was drawing nearer now. Lightning flickered and thunder boomed amongst the rocks of the Crystal Sanctuary. And it seemed to Sammie that something was happening to the crystal too. The green light in the pool was beginning to pulse, as if it was drawing strength from the gathering storm. But the Crystal Keeper had fallen back into a fitful sleep.

Sammie walked softly over and knelt down beside him. Close up, he was even filthier than she had realized. She thought she could see things moving in his hair, and there was a bad smell about his mouldy rags. The idea of having to touch him made her shudder – and when something suddenly wriggled beneath the rags at his throat, she almost cried out in horror.

A moment later, a familiar little brown body popped out. She gave a sigh of relief and watched the mouse scurry to the ground and take up position, like a tiny attendant, at the Crystal Keeper's head. There it sat back and looked up at her solemnly with its beady black eyes and whiskers a-quiver. Please help him, it seemed to be saying.

As Sammie returned its gaze, the Weaver's words came back to her: "…someone who frightens you or who you find disgusting…" and she knew that she had to find the courage somewhere. No one who cared for a little creature like this could be completely wicked.

"I'll do what I can, Mousey," she whispered.

Thinking as hard as she could of her mother and Mere Cottages, she drew a deep breath and reached forward. As if she were touching a cobweb, she placed her palms ever so lightly on the Crystal Keeper's burning forehead. He trembled and gave a great sigh, but his eyes stayed closed. She had no idea whether she was doing the right thing or not. Something just told her to keep her hands on his head and will away his pain. So she screwed her eyes shut and concentrated for all she was worth. It wasn't easy. The ground hurt her knees. Crystal light flickered and lightning flashed against her eyelids. Thunder pealed and cracked overhead. She did her best to ignore it all, but after a while she had to admit that she could concentrate no longer.

As she opened her eyes, something very strange happened. Her head swam and then, to her amazement, she was looking not at the Crystal Keeper but at the Weaver's tapestry. It was dappled with moonlight beneath the great tree on Oak Holm. At its leading edge was a new and unfinished scene. A girl in a filthy white robe knelt beside a sleeping man, her hands on his shaggy head. A tiny mouse looked on. Beside them, a crescent pool of water glowed livid green. Lightning played on the rocky walls around them.

For some time she stared at the tapestry in fascination. Then she looked up to find herself gazing directly into the eyes of the Weaver himself. He was sitting on his stool at the edge of the loom. She couldn't be certain whether he actually saw her, or whether he was staring straight through her.

Behind him were the animals. They too had their eyes fixed on her. But again, she couldn't be sure whether they really saw her. For a moment, as she stared at the old man and his friends, she sensed that something was missing from the scene around the great oak tree.

But then her attention was caught by something quite different. It felt like a stirring inside her, a soft ripple of pure, clean strength that was beginning to wash away her tiredness and fear. And all at once she understood what was happening. The Weaver and his animals were willing her to heal the Crystal Keeper!

The vision of Oak Holm dimmed. The Crystal Keeper shuddered and sighed again. Sammie turned back to him and very gently began to feel his head. His tiny attendant was still there, sitting back on its hind legs, watching her intently. There was something comforting about the beady black eyes and the twitching whiskers, Sammie thought. They made her feel she wasn't completely alone.

She went on probing the Crystal Keeper's head and her fingers soon met a lump, pushing up through the filthy, matted hair. The skin around it was burning hot. She placed her hands around the lump, and as she did so she became aware of a new sensation. There was a strange tingling that began somewhere inside her and ended up in the palms of her hands. It was as if a river of healing power was beginning to flow through her and into the Crystal Keeper's damaged skull.

Now the storm was gathering strength. The Sanctuary flickered with crystal light and teetered crazily with lightning. The wind got up, bringing with it a cold, stinging rain, and within moments Sammie was chilled to the bone. But she closed her mind to it all as the tingling grew more intense and gradually she felt the angry heat leaving the lump. Then, very slowly, the lump itself began to disappear. And while one miracle took place beneath her hands, another was beginning to take place in her heart. Little by little, all her dread and disgust was leaving her and in its place came a feeling of something almost like sympathy for the gaunt, ragged figure at her side.

*   *   *

There was a sudden cry of alarm followed by an almighty crack of thunder. A great blast of wind tore across the Sanctuary. Sammie looked up to see Helio and Jandus staggering backwards towards her. They were bent almost double in the gale, their eyes fixed on the boulders.

Then came a brilliant flash of lightning and through the entrance to the Sanctuary poured the prisoners, with Mick at their head brandishing a length of wood for a club. Hard behind them came Sark and a stream of other snarling, spitting creatures. In the lightning glare, the great sawback's carbuncle eyes glinted hungrily for revenge.

When Mick was nearly level with Sammie, he halted, raising his weapon in the air with a defiant yell. As the prisoners rallied to him, Sammie briefly glimpsed the waif-like figure of Marga amongst them, her face set in grim determination. Then Sark was on them. Mick swung the club like a baseball bat and caught the sawback a furious blow on the side of the head. Sark reeled sideways, then reeled again as Helio lurched forward, face pale and teeth clenched with the effort, to give a one-handed thrust with his dagger. Sammie thought she saw dark blood spurt from the sawback's side, then the creatures and prisoners closed in and the Sanctuary was engulfed in battle.

Above the shouts and cries, the wind rose to a howling fury and the rain came down in an icy, drenching torrent. Sammie crouched shivering beside the crystal pool as the struggle raged before her. Brave as they were, the prisoners were hopelessly out-numbered, and when a fresh wave of creatures burst through the archway, they could resist no longer. Little by little they began to be driven across the Sanctuary towards her.

The battle was almost upon her when there came a new sound. It was the whistle of wind through a thousand wings. She glanced up and her blood ran cold. In the jagged glare of a lightning flash, she could see the dark sky filled with the shadowy forms of birds, twisting, turning and diving down into the fray in a frenzy of stabbing beaks and slashing claws.

So this is the end, she thought, covering her head with her arms. Any moment now it'll all be over. But the tearing, slicing pain never came. She looked up again and saw at once what, in her fear, she had failed to notice at first – that it was the creatures the birds were attacking, not the humans. Then she under-stood what had been missing in her vision of the Weaver and the loom. The birds. Of course. They'd been on their way here!

Now there was a great fluttering as yet more birds

swooped down and hovered in front of her. They were forming themselves into a feathered wall between her and the battle beyond. Sammie gave a silent prayer of thanks to the Weaver. Then she turned again to the Crystal Keeper.

She placed her hands on his head once more, searching for the lump which had now almost vanished. But as she did so she was almost blinded by a sudden flash from the crystal. She rocked backwards and the Crystal Keeper groaned as a second blast of light issued from the crystal. It scattered the hovering birds so that Sammie could see the floor of the Sanctuary beyond, strewn with bodies. The fighting had ended, it seemed. There was nothing and no one left alive.

In horror, she swung her gaze between the battlefield, the crystal pool and the Crystal Keeper. Even the mouse had deserted them now. What was going on?

As if in answer to her question there came a low, angry bubbling sound. She looked over and saw that the water in the crescent pool seemed to be boiling. Somewhere in its depths the crystal had begun to throb, pumping its green light fiercely around the Sanctuary.

Then, very faintly, she sensed Uru trying to speak

to her. She looked across at the cage. There was no sign of life from the great white owl, but little by little, with dreadful effort, he was managing to send his words into her mind:

Poisoned ... he's poisoned ... the crystal ... out of control now ... getting stronger ... soon ... destroy itself ... everything else ... whole valley...

A dull cracking sound began to come from within the rocky pool. A wave broke over the edge and trickled towards the Crystal Keeper. As the water touched his bare arm he screamed and arched his back.

For a moment Sammie's mind went blank with panic. "What do I do? What do I *do*?" she cried out.

And all at once she knew. Leaving the Crystal Keeper where he lay, she stood up and waded out into the pool, stumbling waist-deep towards the very centre, from where the sound seemed to come. Then she leant forward and plunged her arms into the seething water, fumbling blindly for the crystal. The terrible light beat through her in waves but at last her hands closed around a smooth, ice-cold object that quivered so furiously she could scarcely keep hold of it.

With all her might she clung to the crystal and willed the healing power to flow through her one last time, but her senses were so battered that she could no longer feel anything at all. Still the water seethed, the light pulsed and the cracking sound grew louder and louder. Now the crystal shook and shuddered more and more violently, until at last there was a monstrous explosion of sound and light, she felt her hands being blown apart – and then darkness.

Chapter 19

Crystal Keeper's Return

Someone was calling her name.

Sammie opened her eyes to find herself lying on a couch in a warm, spacious tent. Sunlight streamed through the open doorway to frame the figure of Helio who stood before her, smiling broadly. He wore a clean robe, his thick dark hair was brushed and shining, and his broken arm was supported in a newly-folded white sling.

"Helio!" she gasped, sitting up. "Wh-where am I?"

"At the meeting place at the edge of the forest," said Helio, his eyes twinkling. "By the offering stone."

"But ... but ... the battle ... I thought you were..." And she burst into tears.

Helio's face fell. For a moment he stood there awkwardly, then he sat down on the couch and put his good arm around her.

"It's all right," he said gently. "Everything's all right now."

225

"Mick … and Jandus?" Sammie sobbed. "Are they all right, too?"

"Yes. They're both fine. You'll see Mick in a minute."

"And Marga – and all the other prisoners?"

He nodded.

"Oh, Helio," Sammie sniffed, trying to smile through her tears, "I feel so silly … crying when everyone's all right…"

It took a little while for what he had said to sink in properly. And when at last she realized that the danger really was past, she felt a sudden bubbling up of laughter. She laughed and laughed until her whole body heaved uncontrollably with relief and happiness, and Helio was laughing with her, the tears running down his cheeks.

Eventually they stopped and Helio said: "So, shall I tell you what happened?"

Sammie nodded.

"Well," he began, "you saw us when we were fighting in the Sanctuary, didn't you? We were doing our best, but we were starting to lose ground to the creatures – and then the Weaver's birds arrived, thank the Lights! But I didn't see much of what happened after that because I got knocked out. I didn't come round until you were out in the middle of the crystal pool. I could see it all but I knew there was nothing I could do. It was terrible. You looked as if you were going to die. Then there was this gigantic explosion and I passed out again.

"Next thing I knew it was morning. You wouldn't believe what had happened. There was my brother Laslo sitting on the ground in the remains of the cage. Birds were singing and all the swamp creatures had gone. I could hear forest people – the slaves, I suppose – talking and laughing as they started to make their way home. All around the Sanctuary, Jandus and the other prisoners were beginning to come to their senses." He paused, grinning. "And guess what?"

"Tell me."

"There was the Crystal Keeper! He was sound asleep by the crystal pool – just as if nothing had ever happened."

"So we did it!" exclaimed Sammie.

"Yes," said Helio, looking at her intently. "*You* did."

"We both did it," she said, blushing. "In fact all of us – Jandus, Mick, Marga, the other prisoners, everyone. Anyway, what happened then?"

"You were still out for the count," he went on. "You looked terrible. We were pretty worried about you. So we sent one of the prisoners ahead to the castle to let them know what had happened. Then we made up a sort of stretcher out of branches and set off as fast we could, taking turns to carry you. We were nearly at the edge of the forest when we met my mother and father. They reckoned there wasn't time to get you back to the castle, so we made a camp here. Just as well, too. I don't think you'd have lasted much longer."

"I feel fine now," Sammie said.

"You've got my mother and the crystal to thank for that," said Helio with a smile. "It took some fancy spells, I can tell you – and it was still touch and go for a bit. You'd had a dreadful time, you know."

Sammie nodded. She was silent for a while as she thought about everything that had taken place. Then she said: "Helio, what happens now … I mean, now that it's all over?"

"I suppose you'll go back," he said slowly. "Back to Beyond."

"I suppose I will." She paused. "And what about you?"

"Oh, life as normal in the castle…" He tried to sound breezy but she could see his eyes moistening. Then he mumbled: "I'll miss you, Sammie."

"Oh, Helio," she said, her own tears welling again,

"I'll miss you too." She flung her arms around him. This time he hugged her back as tightly as he could with one arm.

"Do you think you'll ever come back?" he asked softly.

"I don't know," she replied. "But I hope so. I really hope so."

Helio broke away again and fumbled in his robe. He held out a velvet pouch.

"Well, whether you do or not, this is something to remember us by."

Sammie felt in the pouch and pulled out a little jewelled rainbow on a golden chain.

"The Rainbow of Lights!" she cried, seeing how it sparkled even in the soft light inside the tent. But as she held it up to her throat, her skin suddenly felt strangely naked. For an instant she couldn't think why. Then it dawned on her that the little fishbone owl was no longer there. Her face fell.

"Don't you like it?" asked Helio anxiously.

"Oh, yes," she said, looking admiringly again at the rainbow. "It's beautiful, really it is. But – I seem to have lost my little Uru carving. The one he got Jandus to make for me."

Helio smiled again and shook his head knowingly. "You haven't lost it, Sammie. It just – doesn't exist any more … now that my brother's no longer an owl. Don't ask me how … we don't understand everything the crystal does… Anyway, you've got the Rainbow of Lights instead. Put it on. There! It looks lovely!"

"Oh, Helio," said Sammie, fastening the clasp, "it *is* lovely! Really lovely! Thank you!"

Helio stood up. "You get dressed now. We've got one more thing to do."

"What?" asked Sammie.

"Not telling!" said Helio with a mischievous grin. He left the tent.

Sammie rose from the couch and pulled on the clean white robe that was draped over a nearby stool. She glanced down at herself and realized that all the grime from the last few days had gone. Her skin was pink and scrubbed and her hair hung soft and shiny around her face. Wondering what was coming next, she stepped into the sunshine.

The first person she saw was Mick, waiting just outside the entrance of the tent. With the dark curls poking out from under his back-to-front cap, the round wire-framed spectacles, a gleaming white robe and a grin that stretched from ear to ear, he looked more than ever like something out of a cartoon. He didn't say anything as she came out, just kept grinning and slipped his arm through hers. A moment later Helio appeared and took her other arm, and together they led her along between two rows of tents.

Turning the corner at the last tent, Sammie stopped and blinked in amazement. Ahead of them, bathed in late afternoon sunlight, the great marble offering stone glistened against its dark forest backdrop. Stretching down towards it, dressed in their finest clothes, were two long lines of people from the town and castle, an avenue of smiling faces and hands poised for applause.

Helio and Mick led her forward and a great cheer went up. Sammie felt a lump rise in her throat. She floated dizzily along as hands reached out for hers and a hundred voices congratulated her. It must be a dream, said a part of her, while another part longed to go on walking down this wonderful avenue for ever. Then they were nearing the end. There, standing a little apart, was the tall, stooping figure of the Master. Beside him, short and plump, stood the Dame. And there was a third person Sammie didn't recognize.

"My dear!" The Dame's voice bubbled with pleasure as she drew Sammie to her comfortable bosom and hugged her so tight Sammie could hardly breathe. "Oh, my dear, I knew you could do it. I just *knew* you could!" She sounded for a moment like an excited schoolgirl.

Then the Master was bending forward, silver-haired and smiling, to take her hands in his. "I don't know how we'll ever thank you, Sammie," he said, his eyes creasing with pride and gratitude.

"And neither do I," said the stranger solemnly, stepping up to make a little bow. "But I promise you one thing – you'll never have to come flying with me again!"

Sammie let out a squeak of delight. "Ur – I mean – Laslo!"

"The very same!" said Laslo, flapping his arms. A wicked twinkle crept into his deep blue eyes and for a moment, thought Sammie, he could almost have been Helio's twin.

"Well now," said the Master, taking her by the hand again, "we have a little ceremony starting in a minute or two. I think you'll enjoy it. So come and take your seat, my dear."

A semi-circle of chairs had been set out facing the offering stone. The Master led Sammie to the place of honour in the very centre, then showed Helio and Mick to their places on either side of her. Behind them, there was a growing murmur as a great crowd began to gather. Sammie turned round and was delighted to notice familiar faces amongst the throng. There stood the captains and crews of both the ships. Over there were the prisoners from World's Edge, amongst them the elfin figure of Marga. Her huge grey eyes met Sammie's and she smiled and gave a hesitant little nod. Then Sammie's attention was caught by a shock of white hair bobbing along through the crowd. A few seconds later, out popped the Weaver, his tattered red cloak flapping as he hurried up to take his place in the front row, next to Laslo. He gave her a cheery wave and an "I-told-you-so" wink as he sat down. And there, scarcely recognizable in a brand new tunic, was Jandus, all overcome with pride as the Master showed him to his seat on the other side of Laslo. Sammie caught his eye and a shy smile flitted across his nutbrown face.

She sank back happily into her chair, already beginning to feel sleepy again. The shadows were lengthening now, but the air was still warm and there was a pleasant buzz of voices around her. On one side, Helio was deep in conversation with his brother. On the other side, Mick was talking to the Dame, grinning like a hyena. And as Sammie heard the Dame exclaim for the umpteenth time how brave he was, she realized drowsily that that was all Mick had ever really wanted from the start – to do something that would get people making a fuss of him…

Eventually the sun set and the Master walked out to the offering stone. Sammie's eyes were beginning to grow heavy as she heard him speak to the crowd of "Sammie, the brave Beyonder … saviour of our valley…" and "Mick, the wolf-slayer … her valiant stepbrother…"

She dimly heard him call for the Crystal Keeper to come forth, and the echoing roar of the crowd drummed in her ears like distant surf.

And then, as if in a waking dream, she felt a great rush of pride and delight as out from amongst the trees strode a tall, handsome figure in a robe of deep forest-green, on whose shoulder, whiskers twitching and bright eyes gleaming, perched a little brown mouse.

She watched in wonder as he drew level with the offering stone and bowed graciously to the Master. Then he turned, and she blushed deeply as he smiled a solemn smile and, to a great roar of approval from the crowd, bowed to her too. And though she still only half believed what she was seeing, as he held out a tiny phial of clear, sparkling crystal and placed it on the offering stone, she found herself murmuring under her breath:

234

"It was all worth it! It was all definitely worth it!"

But even as she said it, her eyelids drooped again, and this time she had no will to resist.

And when, a moment later, the Master took the little phial from the stone, placed it in his robe, and stepped forward to embrace the Crystal Keeper, Sammie did not notice.

For she was sound asleep.

Chapter 20

Rainbow's End

An explosion thudded through the darkness. It was followed by the roar and crackle of flames.

Sammie scrambled to her feet in confusion. Where was she? At the Crystal Sanctuary? By the offering stone?

Now she could see a dull red glow through the trees ahead of her. There was a smell of burning timber. She set off towards the blaze at a trot. In the flickering darkness she stumbled into a rhododendron bush and all at once she knew where she was.

In the wood at home! Looking for Mick! But hang on … hadn't the mere been right in front of her? Here there was nothing but undergrowth. So where was she? What was going on…?

As she pondered this there was another *whoosh* and a fireworks display of sparks sailed into the night sky. She began to get the nasty feeling that Mick had something to do with all this, and all at once she remembered the funny smell and the singed eyebrows when he'd turned up on Oak Holm. Yes. This was definitely Mick's handiwork. She broke into a run and soon the outline of some kind of shed became visible ahead. It was engulfed in flames.

"Mick!" she yelled in panic. "Mick! Where are you? Can you hear me?"

But the roaring and crackling was so loud that even if he had replied she wouldn't have heard him. A furnace blast of heat met her and she skidded to a halt, unable to approach any closer.

She was beside the mere, not hers – but the other, real one. Directly in front of her, blazing like an inferno, stood the boathouse.

"Mick!" she yelled again, but there was no reply. She dashed to one side of the boathouse and peered into the flames. The ancient timbers burned so fiercely that she could see nothing beyond them. She could smell her own hair starting to singe now as she raced round to the other side. Then there was a loud crack and a frenzy of sparks as the roof collapsed and part of the wall fell in with it. Flaming planks hissed as they met the water and a cloud of steam filled the gap in the wall.

As the steam cleared, Sammie peered inside, dreading what she might see. But there was no crumpled figure there, neither on the ground nor in the rowing boat that rocked gently in the smouldering, plank-tangled dock. Then there was a groan as the rest of the boathouse fell in on itself, and in the final blaze of flame she noticed a movement on the mere. She stepped back for a better look and her heart stopped. Turning a gentle circle on the still, dark water was a green baseball cap.

Sammie felt the panic rushing back. She dashed to the bank and without stopping to remove her shoes or sweatshirt, leapt into the mere, gasping as she plunged down through the deep, cold water. She surfaced and trod water for a moment to catch her breath, then duck-dived into the darkness. Down she went, kicking with all her strength as the water grew colder and the pressure began to drum at her ears. But she failed to touch the bottom and eventually she had to shoot to the surface, gasping for air. Again and again she went down until at last she could dive no more. Clutching the baseball cap, she paddled back to the bank and clung there, sobbing and panting with exhaustion and despair.

Oh, Mick, she thought. And all because of a stupid crystal in some other world. What a way for it to end…

Then something caught her eye. Lying in the

shadows a little way along the bank was a log-like shape, at one end of which two discs glinted in the dying light of the fire.

With chattering teeth, Sammie heaved herself out of the water and stood up. At that instant the log gave a loud groan. She stumbled along the bank on wobbly legs and stopped, a few paces further on, by the tree root over which Mick must have tripped in the darkness. For a moment she felt like screaming at having got so cold and wet for nothing. Then the relief began to take hold and she started to shake.

He must have banged his head pretty hard, she thought, squatting down beside him in the shadows. Drips from her hair and sodden clothes pattered down on him but he remained motionless, even though the reflection of the firelight in his spectacles made it look as if his eyelids might be fluttering. Presumably, he'd knocked over the paraffin lamp, then started to run when the boathouse went up. She glanced back at the remains of the wooden shed and the dark trees around it, and thanked goodness for all that rain there'd been.

Then an odd feeling intruded on her thoughts, a very faint stirring inside her. The palms of her hands began to tingle softly. Before she'd even realized what was going on, she was reaching out to feel his head, gently probing his skull with her fingers, searching the scalp for any signs of damage…

Mick gave another loud groan, rolled away from her and sat up. He shook his head and peered about, but he seemed unable to focus properly. His expression was confused and disorientated, as if he'd just slept for a week and didn't know where he was. But eventually he caught sight of the glowing embers and their dim reflection in the mere.

"Oh, no," he muttered, raising his eyes in dismay.

For a while, he stared at the smouldering ruin in silence, then let his head fall forward on to his knees. He gave no sign of having even noticed Sammie.

She was quite unprepared when he suddenly sat up again and said coldly: "Why are you here?"

"Wh-what?" Sammie stammered.

"I *said* why are you here?"

Sammie's heart sank. Was it possible, despite everything that had happened in the valley, that nothing had really changed at all?

"I … I…" she began but Mick cut her off with a scowl.

"I s'pose you were following me."

Sammie felt the familiar anger rising. She was on the point of replying: Yes, dead right I was following you, and a good thing too, as it turns out – when she had a sudden thought. She took a grip on herself and said instead:

"Listen, Mick. D'you know where we've just been – you and I?"

He glared at her suspiciously and for a horrible moment she thought he was going to ask what on earth she was talking about. She held her breath. Then gradually something changed in his face and a faraway look came into his eyes. He stared out across the dark water for a long time before eventually giving the slightest nod.

"You remember?"

"Yes." It was almost a whisper.

"All of it?"

"Yes."

"Well, shall I tell you something, Mick?"

"Okay."

"You – were – utterly – brilliant!"

He looked up. Very slowly, a grin spread across his face. "Know what?" he said.

"What?"

"You weren't so bad yourself!"

Life quickly returned to normal at number 3, Mere Cottages.

When he heard what had happened, Mick's father

was so relieved that no one had been hurt and the wood hadn't been set on fire, that he wasn't angry for long. He docked Mick's pocket money for a donation to the local angling club who owned the boathouse – but even they weren't too upset about it all, because the boathouse had been old and rotten and they were about to pull it down anyway and build a new one.

"So you saved them the bother," said his father, shaking his head. "Well, well. You'll not pull a stunt like that again, will you?"

"No, Dad," said Mick. And it was quite obvious to everyone that he meant it.

For her part, Sammie was glad it was all over. She rode her bike, read, listened to music and found herself grateful to be doing ordinary, everyday things that didn't involve having to be brave.

But the memory of the valley remained inside her like a continual glow. She would throw open the doors to it last thing at night, before she went to sleep, or during a lazy moment in the garden.

Then she would see Helio's mischievous look as he peered round the cabin door, or Jandus grinning lopsidedly in his little boat, or the birds and animals around the loom, or the Weaver twinkling at her from beneath his amazing eyebrows.

But for all the happy memories, there was one

thing that saddened her. The little jewelled rainbow had vanished.

A day or two later, she and Mick searched all around the remains of the boathouse, but without success.

"It must've come off when I was diving," she said sadly as they walked back to the house. "I s'pose I'll have to forget about it."

Mick nodded sympathetically.

The next day Sammie went shopping with her mother and Mick spent the morning in the garden shed.

When he emerged at lunchtime it was to present her with a small parcel, done up with some old birthday wrapping paper.

"What's this?" she asked.

Mick winked. "Surprise! Open it. Go on!"

She undid the wrapping to reveal a small, rather uneven wooden rainbow, painted in wobbly lines with model aeroplane paint. Mick grinned happily as Sammie fastened the two pieces of string which held it around her neck.

"Oh, Mick," she said, trying not to laugh. "Thanks ever so much! It's lovely!"

That evening, as Sammie was getting ready for bed,

there was a knock on the door and her mother came in.

She sat down on the edge of the bed and watched as Sammie finished folding her clothes and brushed her hair. She was obviously in the mood for a chat.

As Sammie hopped into bed, her mother spotted the rainbow lying on the bedside table. "What on earth's that?" she asked.

"Mick made it for me," Sammie replied.

"Hmmm…" mused her mother. "You two are best friends all of a sudden, aren't you? Mick – he's being so … nice. I can hardly believe it. And you're different too … you've changed … least it seems you have." She looked at her daughter directly. "What's going on?"

Sammie thought for a long moment. Then she pulled her knees up under her chin and said: "The weirdest thing happened to me, Mum. You remember that dream you had, the one about the little brown man and the white bird?"

Her mother nodded.

"Well," Sammie continued, "it's to do with that. I don't really expect you'll believe me, but I want to tell you anyway…"

So she told the whole story, from beginning to end. It was past midnight when she finished.

"So that's why Mick made me the rainbow," she concluded.

For a moment they sat in silence. Sammie found it hard to tell from her mother's expression whether she believed her or not. She didn't really like to ask.

Then her mother got to her feet and said: "I'll be back in a minute."

She went out of the room and Sammie heard the floorboards creaking in the passage.

Shortly she reappeared. She was holding a twist of tissue paper which she gave to Sammie without a word.

Sammie opened it and gasped to see a jewelled rainbow on a gold chain. It was identical to the one that Helio had given her.

Before she could speak, her mother smiled gently and said:

"It belonged to your grandmother. I always wondered where it came from. Now I know."

Animal Rescue by **Bette Paul**

Tessa finds life in the country *so* different from life in
the town. Will she ever be accepted? But everything
changes when she meets Nora and Ned who run the
village animal sanctuary, and becomes involved in a
struggle to save the badgers of Delves Wood
from destruction . . .

Thunderfoot by **Deborah van der Beek**

Mel Whitby has always loved horses, and when she
comes across an enormous by neglected horse in a
railway field, she desperately wants to take care of it.
But little does she know that taking care of
Thunderfoot will change her life forever . . .

A Foxcub Named Freedom by **Brenda Jobling**

A vixen lies seriously injured in the undergrowth. Her
young son comes to her for comfort and warmth. The
cub wants to help his mother to safety, but it is
impossible. The vixen, sensing danger, nudges him
away, caring nothing for herself – only for
his freedom . . .

The Babysitters Club

Need a babysitter? Then call the Babysitters Club. Kristy Thomas and her friends are all experienced sitters. They can tackle any job from rampaging toddlers to a pandemonium of pets. To find out all about them, read on!